I0630321

No Other Magic Necessary

Sylvan Valley, Volume 1

Solara Gordon

Published by THE EARTH MOVED, LLC, 2025.

This is a work of fiction. Similarities to real people, places, or events are entirely coincidental.

NO OTHER MAGIC NECESSARY

First edition. May 15, 2025.

Copyright © 2025 Solara Gordon.

ISBN: 979-8991796286

Written by Solara Gordon.

Also by Solara Gordon

Sylvan Valley
No Other Magic Necessary

Standalone
A Heart's Desire
To Love You Again
To Love You Again

Watch for more at https://solaragordon.com/.

With every book, there are inspirations, helpers and those that enjoy the simple story as your write it. The first draft and concept are always for the author/writer.

My Inspiration came from watching a Bewitched reruns. A what if story idea formed taking bits and pieces from my Cauldron Falls series and Cauldron Falls-Sylvan Valley Founding Families series.

Many thanks goes to Chevy Allen, my beta reader and LOL moment partner as I wrote No Other Magic Necessary.

I hope you enjoy Evan and Aprell's journey to their second chance at love plus their family and extended family members second chances at love.

Happy Reading, Loving, and Laughter,

Solara Gordon

CHAPTER ONE

"What do you mean I've got to give up spellcasting?" Maxi Waller faced her coven sisters, Tabby Nichols and Donya Alvarez.

Tabby moved closer, slipping her arm around Maxi's waist. "Nobody wants to give up. But darlin', your last love potion damn near had Mr. Smithson serenading St. Michael's new minister's wife. Not good if you ask me."

"One bad love potion doesn't make me a wash-up." Maxi sighed, hugged Tabby and glanced at Donya.

Donya stepped closer to her. "Maxi, face it. Sooner or later, we get to a point where twitching and witching aren't our best skills." Donya pointed to her nose, trying to twitch it quickly.

Maxi pressed her lips together, hoping to hide her grin. The only thing Donya moved back and forth quickly were her puckered lips as she stared almost cross-eyed at her nose. She finally used her finger to push her nose back and forth.

Tabby snorted. "Donya, your twitching stopped right after you broke your nose playing basketball with Evan. How you kept up with him is beyond me."

Donya smiled. "Evan is his father's son through and through. Athletic, mortal and non-magical!"

"Evan's a damn fine doctor if you ask me. Not bad looking either." Maxi pointed at the cast covering her arm from elbow to wrist. "He took me to the emergency room and stayed with me until the orthopedist took over."

"If you hadn't been trying to show Mr. Yost's grandson how to ride his skateboard, you wouldn't have fallen off it as you hit that uneven patch of sidewalk on Main Street." Tabby reached for Maxi's purse. "Where did you stash your keys?"

"Did I put them in here or in my pocket?" Maxi shook her purse with her good arm. She listened for the sound of metal jingling. Nothing. Patting her pockets, she felt for the bulge, indicating which one held her keys.

"Dang, Did I leave them at the hospital?" Maxi closed her eyes, trying to remember if she even locked her door before Evan had rushed her to the emergency room.

"Maxi, another reason you've got to stop living alone. At two hundred, we're not as spry as we used to be, nor is our memory as good. Let me have your purse." Donya eased the heavy bag off Maxi's arm.

"Goddess above, what is in this?" Donya grasped the purse with two hands. "How you carry this is beyond me."

Tabby guided Maxi up her front steps and onto the porch bench. "Come on, Donya. If she's got what I think she's got in there, you're gonna have to empty part of it out to find much of anything useful."

Tabby helped Maxi sit down. Turning to Donya, Tabby rolled her eyes. Tabby knew getting Maxi to slow down and give up her half-assed spells wouldn't be easy.

As Donya sat the purse down on the bench, Maxi jolted upright. "I know who has my keys. Evan does. He grabbed them as he took my purse off the counter. I bet he's still got them. I remember him locking up as I tried putting on my sweater."

Donya glanced down into the purse's interior. By the porch light, she could make out part of the contents. A wadded-up sweater, a small wand, two bottles of bespelled water and a large can of mace. She pushed the bag open further, peering inside. At the bottom, she saw two large bricks and Maxi's wallet. What in Goddess's name were the bricks for? Shaking her head, Donya faced Maxi. "I'm not going to ask. Just suggest you not carry so much weight in here for a while. If you feel you need extra protection, get a guard dog. You've been without a familiar too long."

Maxi leaned back against the bench's back and sighed. "Right now, all I want is to feel my bed cradling me as I sleep. Evan is supposed to bring me some pain meds when he gets home. What time is it?"

Tabby glanced at her watch. "Almost seven. What time did he say he'd be home?"

Donya pulled a crumpled piece of paper with writing on it out of her pants pocket. She smoothed it out as best she could. Holding it up to the porch light, she squinted at the writing.

Tabby pulled it from Donya's hand. "You forget your glasses? Again?"

Donya sheepishly shrugged and nodded. "Guess each of us needs to keep an eye on the other."

Tabby moved under the porch light and read. "I'll be home around seven. Keep Maxi comfortable and upright. The pain pills I'm prescribing will help her sleep. In the morning, bring her to my office for a follow-up x-ray. The swelling will be down enough by then."

The three witches turned as a red sports car pulled up in front of Maxi's house. A tall, dark-haired male got out. His hair stood up in places. The rolled-up sleeves of his light-colored shirt stopped partway up his forearms. Dark pants completed his outfit. As he got closer, Donya smiled. Evan would make sure Maxi slept through the night. In the morning, she and Tabby would explain why they'd called Maxi's granddaughter, Aprell Stallings.

Evan Gladstone trotted up the walkway. He could see his grandmother, Donya, hovering over her friend. Abada, as he called her, worried about her coven sisters. Abada's coven sisters were his Tias by choice. Extended family that accepted him and cared for him.

Evan knew Abada's coven sisters were her sole link to her magical community. He called them her church group since his paternal grandparents and relatives didn't understand magic. To them, it belonged in movies and television. Evan knew firsthand about magic. Abada had taught him small tricks and sleight-of-hand that most beginning magicians could do, not him. He loved that she never looked down on him or treated him differently due to his non-magical ability.

Evan bound up the steps stopping beside his grandmother. He kissed her cheek. "Te quiero Abada. How's my patient doing?"

Donya kissed his cheek and faced him. "Maxi is holding her own. I hope you brought the pain pills and her keys."

Evan chuckled. Tia Maxi, his elderly landlord, could forget the littlest things. Her stories of her younger days as a witch in her prime were full of details and nuances. He wished he didn't have to call Aprell to help with moving her to the Witches Relief Society home. But today's fall showed Maxi needed guidance and care that living alone wasn't providing her.

He reached into his pocket and pulled out two sets of keys. Handing the large letter M keychain to his grandmother, he stuffed his car keys back in his pocket. "I called Maxi's prescription into the local all-night pharmacy. They'll deliver the medication in about an hour. Meanwhile, get her in bed with some fluids and a lite meal. Bring her to the office tomorrow morning for another x-ray. With the swelling down, the orthopedist and I can tell if more than a hairline fracture is involved."

Donya nodded. She reached up and patted his cheek. "Te quiero tambien. Tabby and I will stay here tonight. Be good and bring over some of the clothes I left at your place the last time I visited. Tabby and I are about the same size. We'll be fine for tomorrow."

Tabby rose from where she sat on the bench next to Maxi. "Evan, can you do me a favor and call my niece to take care of Aloysius for a couple of days?"

Evan snorted. "That mangy old fleabag is still around? I'm glad you're asking her to take care of him. He tried to bite me last time I got near him."

Tabby laughed. "Yes, he's still with me. He's fathered a few replacements since you last saw him. I suspect he's a bit mellower now. He's minus a few things if you know what I mean."

Evan burst out laughing at Tabby's conspirator wink. "I bet ole Al wasn't too happy when that happened."

"Vet said a cat his age had no business fucking as much as Al tried to do with picking fights with the younger tom cats in the neighborhood."

Evan bit his lip to keep from laughing out loud more. He could see the old, thin black tomcat egging the younger ones on. His notched ears weren't due to surgery. One vet swore he'd never seen so many jagged tears and bites as Al had in his heyday. "Tabby, I'll make sure Al is looked after and *not* by me."

"Thank you. I appreciate you doing that." Tabby assisted Maxi to her feet. "Donya and I will make sure Maxi gets to bed. You can call before you bring the things over. I'll keep an ear out for the pharmacy delivery. "

Evan moved closer to Maxi. Her semi-closed eyes indicated the last shot he'd given her at the emergency room was taking full effect. She'd doze until the other meds arrived. He doubted she'd need them but wanted to be sure she slept soundly. Sleep and food would do her good. She'd lost some weight since the last time he'd seen her a month ago. Maybe she needed care that living alone she wasn't getting. He felt terrible for not looking after her better.

"Tia Maxi, I want you to get into bed. Listen to Abada and Tia Tabby. Nothing else. Eat lightly and go to sleep. Promise me you'll behave." Evan leaned down and kissed her cheek. "I need my beauty sleep, too. Can't be scaring my patients looking bleary-eyed and scowling."

Tia Maxi's weak smile told him she was falling asleep fast. Good, he knew that a bit of food would help the meds ward off more pain and get her into slumber without him having to worry.

Evan hugged his grandmother and whispered to her. "Abada, some broth and toast will be good. I doubt she'll get much down her. Half a cup of broth and a piece of toast will be fine. I'll be back with the clothes in about twenty minutes."

Evan caught his grandmother's nod as he hurried back down the stairs and across the front lawn toward the four-unit apartment building Maxi owned next door.

Donya smiled as Evan jogged over the lawn and jumped over the small retaining wall separating the two yards. "That boy has a heart of gold and love. I wish he'd find someone to settle down with."

"How about Aprell?" Tabby clapped her hand over her mouth as soon as she spoke. Now she'd done it. Spilled the surprise. *Shit*, now Maxi would be fussing and fuming. She hated calling her granddaughter. Maxi swore the only time she'd call Aprell was if she needed watching and chaperoning. Well, the poor dear needed help. And obviously, a bit of watching. As long as Maxi stayed away from Mr. Yost, the two needed no chaperones. Get the two in the same range and look out. Maybe Yost was an old mage in disguise.

Inside his apartment, Evan searched through two closets before he found the suitcase and box he wanted. The box was marked in bold letters, *Evan Stay Out.* He suspected the box held the bras, panties and nightgowns Abada wanted. He knew she had several pairs of pants and tops in the suitcase. Evan smiled as he tucked the box under one arm. What if he cut the tape on the box enough to indicate he may have looked inside? Ooh, what a fuss Abada would make. If Tia Maxi weren't hurt, he'd do it. He was long overdue to pull a prank on Abada.

Don't even think about it, Evan.

Evan turned around as he reached the door. "Abada?" He gazed at the mirror over his fireplace. She'd sworn she'd dispelled the place after her last visit.

No image greeted him. *Whoosh*—-Evan heaved a sigh of relief. Good, she didn't know about the two nurses he'd brought home a couple nights ago.

I do now. His grandmother's laughter echoed in his mind.

Blast it, Abada! Stop reading my mind. You might not like what you find.

Stop fretting. I wanted to tell you the pharmacy delivered. Maxi ate and passed out. Hurry up as Tabby and I are ready to fall on our faces as you say.

Be right there.

Evan chuckled as he locked his door. Leave it to Abada to sneak up on him. He laughed as he trotted back across the lawn. Good thing he learned to shield or Abada would be red-faced at his memories of the two nurses.

"Maxi missed my reference to Aprell." Tabby glanced over her shoulder at Maxi's partially closed bedroom door.

"Oh, she heard you. I caught her wide-eyed stare before you turned back. She'll blast us in the morning. Too late by then. I'm calling Aprell now." Donya picked up her cell phone and thumbed through her contacts until she located Aprell's number. Glancing at the large wall clock near the front door, Donya calculated the time difference to Hawaii where Aprell lived. Two rings later, Aprell answered.

"Charms and Spells. How can I betwixt you?" Aprell's warm voice came through the phone speaker clearly.

"Hi, Aprell. Tia Donya here." A hard knock sounded at the front door. "Excuse me one moment, Aprell." Donya clicked the mute button and motioned toward the door. "Tabby, can you get that? I'm going into the kitchen to finish talking to Aprell. Thanks."

Tabby rose as Donya pushed open the kitchen door. Great, she had to deal with Evan. Hmm, wonder if he had called her niece yet. She could make small conversation until Donya sent Evan on his way. Tabby stifled a yawn as she opened the door.

Evan's huge grin told her he was up to something. "Want to pull a prank on Abada?" His slight nod and glance around the room said he had it planned out.

Tabby looked over her shoulder. The kitchen door swung back and forth as its movement slowed. "Evan, you are bad!" Tabby shook her finger at him. "What you got in mind?"

Evan moved into the room, closing the door behind him. "Slit the tape on the box marked *stay out* and let Abada think I pawed through it. She'll sputter and spit for a few moments. Then tell her I put you up to it. She'll laugh and chastise me tomorrow."

Tabby blinked her eyes and grinned. "Now you know I will get chastised too. How do you plan on making amends?" She batted her eyes at Evan.

"Tia Tabby, you know I'll make amends. But don't ask how for now. I need sleep, too." Evan yawned and stretched. He placed the box on the coffee table along with the suitcase. "Tell Abada good night for me. I'm off to heat up some dinner and catch up on my email."

Tabby called out as he got to the door. "Remember my niece and Al, okay?"

Evan waved as he opened the door. "That old tom will be fine. I'll call right away. Don't need him haunting my dreams."

CHAPTER TWO

Aprell Stallings opened the suitcase and small duffel bag sitting on her bed. Tia Donya didn't call often. True to Aprell's sinking feeling, something was wrong.

When Tia Donya explained why they needed her help for an indefinite period and where Evan fit in, Aprell knew she couldn't say no. Her family needed her. Well, her family and one pain-in-the-ass male, as she remembered him from his teens. How many years had it been since they'd last seen each other? Possibly ten years. Praise the powers-that-be, the shop was doing well, and she could leave her business partner Nancy Bluestone in charge.

Aprell tossed clothes and shoes into the suitcase. In the duffel, she carefully packed her healing crystals with two books on natural medicine and crystal healing magic. Returning to her closet, she pulled out a tote bag. She placed the small duffel bag inside the tote, along with a few magazines and a book. With one last glance around the room, she took in each item. Her multicolored bedspread from Mexico stood out against her Hawaiian print sheets. She loved colors. Every time she worked with her crystals, she knew she'd made the right choice for her magic tools.

As an empath, she understood everything pulsed with energy and gave off vibrations that enhanced its aura. Each color had its own hot and cold temperature range. She could feel the differences in temperature as she touched or focused on each person or object. Often, the dullest color in the person's aura was where they needed healing. Working with a local naturopath doctor had opened up avenues of clients she wouldn't have known about. Many came into the shop for aura readings, tarot card readings, herbal teas, and aromatherapy items.

Aprell placed the tote and suitcase by the front door. Her plane ticket was waiting for her at the airport. The six-hour flight from Honolulu to Nashville would allow her to sleep and relax. Another two hours by car would bring her to Sylvan Valley.

"Yes, Ms. Stallings, your ticket shows first class. In fact, your aunt paid for concierge service once you reached Nashville. Have a good trip. You board through gate 10B concourse C." The airline attendant stapled her baggage claim check to her ticket folder and slid it toward her. Aprell looked at the boarding pass sticking out of the top flap. Seat 2A stood out in bold, easy-to-read print. How much more coincidence did she need? The numbers 10 and 2 and the flight number 88 might leave superstitious people with an eerie feeling. The numbers representing her birthday, October 2, 1988, brought her luck practically every time she encountered them.

"Thank you," Aprell murmured, picking up the ticket folder and her tote. By the time she got through security and snagged a snack, the walk to the gate would put her about twenty minutes out from boarding.

As she joined the line at the security checkpoint, one thought ran through her mind. This trip wasn't just a visit. This time, change was coming, and not just for her grandmother. Aprell chafed her arms as she exited the metal detector and slipped on her shoes. She softly said a quick prayer. "Keep me safe, Goddess. Gods, add your skill to the pilots that fly me home. Help Grandmother and me through this time of change. Praises be, and blessed am I. Thank you for all you do. Amen."

Aprell settled into her seat and finished the cookie and herbal tea she snagged at the coffee shop as the flight attendants secured the plane door and began the safety announcements. She hoped the two valerian tablets she took would help lull her to sleep.

Aprell yawned and raised her arms over her head. She'd taken the offered pillow and blanket an hour into her flight. Her weird, intermittent dreams made her grin. Nancy, her business partner, had a difficult client demanding fung-shui for every nook and cranny of their new vacation home. Somewhere mixed in with the maddening discussion they had in her last dream, Evan had shown up. Why had he decided to serenade her in some strange language as she tried to calm Nancy and her clients, she couldn't figure out. She knew that taking antihistamines over the counter before flying along with eating sugary food wasn't a good idea. She pushed the overhead call button. Water and tea would dilute the remaining sugar surging through her.

"Yes, ma'am." The steward beamed down at her. Shit, her seat was still reclined. Oh, well. He was probably married with three kids and another on the way. He worked this job to get away from them. Oops, shouldn't judge the poor guy. Just because that was the last line she'd fallen for before she found out the bastard had a woman in practically every mainland major hub.

"I'd like some water and tea. Are there any snacks left?" Aprell reached for the lever to bring her seat upright.

"We'll be serving breakfast soon. I can get you some nuts."

"That's fine. Thank you." The steward nodded and left.

Flying first class was a new experience for her. Tia Donya and Tia Tabby wouldn't hear of saving money or taking economy class. They could afford the ticket. After they'd put her groggy grandmother on the phone, Aprell knew better than to argue more. Her grandmother needed her. Nancy had practically kicked her out the door of the store. So here she sat at thirty-five thousand feet in the air, racing toward Nashville.

Laying the blanket and pillow on the empty seat beside her, Aprell hunched her shoulders and neck. She needed to stand up and freshen up. As she rose, she glanced about the cabin. Several other passengers slept or watched the video entertainment. She was glad no one sat next to her. The extra room allowed her to stretch out in comfort. Sleep had eluded her for several nights the past week.

Aprell clicked the small bathroom door closed behind her. Harsh lights hid nothing. Her hair stood out in places. Her eyes were less bloodshot. She quickly brushed her hair and pulled it back into a low ponytail. She wet a disposable face cloth, working the sweet-smelling lather over her arms and neck. As much as she hated ruining her makeup, her eyes burned. Contacts needed to come out. Makeup off was her only choice. Ten minutes later, she returned to her seat and settled in for the rest of the flight.

Evan clicked on the x-ray viewer as he pulled the x-ray file to him. Maxi's chipper mood and curiosity during her office visit indicated she'd slept well and wasn't groggy from any meds. When he'd asked her about needing a refill, she'd grinned and flirted with him. Evan smiled as he remembered what she'd said.

"Evan, if I were a hundred fifty years younger, I'd give you a run for your money, young man. Remember, age is not always what the body shows; mind over matter helps too." Maxi winced as she moved her casted arm.

"Take it easy, Tia Maxi. I'm not sure you'll heal as fast as you did at a spry one hundred. A healthy mental state does wonders. I want you to slack off on skateboard rides down uneven sidewalks, okay?" Evan pushed the x-ray he held into the viewer. Crap, not as good as he had hoped. Tia Maxi had two hairline fractures in her wrist and forearm. The swelling indicated she bruised ligaments as well. He didn't think she'd sprained anything more than her bruised pride. Lord, he was in big trouble if she was as feisty as Abada.

He pulled the x-ray out of the viewer and clicked the machine off. Picking up the envelope, he eyed the room's other occupants, Tia Tabby and Abada. The looks on their faces said they were waiting. He knew the news he had to deliver wouldn't be easy.

Six to eight weeks in a cast followed by four weeks of physical therapy before Maxi could regain full use of her wrist and arm. He didn't like the bruise marks he saw on her legs and knees. She'd taken quite a spill. He suspected her uneven gait masked a bit of pain and soreness in her hips and back. His next-door neighbor ran a mobile massage therapy business. Maybe she'd be willing to take Tia Maxi on as a client for him. Getting Tia Maxi to see an orthopedist would be akin to getting Tia Tabby's damn tomcat Al to stop humping every female cat he came across, even minus his balls.

"Abada, stop giving me that look." Evan fought to resist the urge to pull at his collar. Ever since he could remember, all Abada had to do was look at him in that tone of voice where if she spoke, her pitch and words would have said he was in deep trouble. Of course, she'd introduced him to the words the first time she'd spanked him. Thank Gods and Goddesses, she'd also told him that he'd have to learn how witches punished their children. He was glad he couldn't feel the power ripple accompanying the look.

"What look is that Evan?" Donya's voice grated like fingernails down a chalkboard as it reached his ears. How did he react without looking like a fool to his nursing assistant who just entered the room?

"Abada, could I please talk to you out in the hall?" Evan nodded toward the door and glared at his grandmother. He knew she'd back down with other mortals present. She restricted her magic when others couldn't defend themselves or understand what was happening.

Donya rose from the chair next to Maxi. "Yes, Evan. One moment, please."

Her smug look sent chills over his shoulders, yet it sparked more ire in his gut. He loved her and knew she wanted the best for her friend. This wasn't magic. He practiced medicine with his hands and heart. Hands-on and a genuine love for healing people. Helping them to find peace even if they couldn't be completely cured left him feeling fulfilled and knowing he'd done all he could. He doubted Abada fully understood. Magic was as natural to her as breathing. Somehow, he needed to get her on the same page. No magic, and let him do what he knew how to do in his sleep. Practice medicine.

Abada leaned down and appeared to be talking to Tia Maxi. What now? Evan shook his head and walked to the door. "Tia Maxi, Tia Tabby can help you get up on the table. I want to check out your legs to be sure they didn't bruise more than what I saw in the ER last night."

He caught Tia Maxi's slight nod as he turned. " Tia Tabby, Al is fine. He's at your niece's ruling the roost with her feline. Her poor Chihuahua is cowering under the couch."

Tia Tabby's snort and laugh made him smile as he stepped out into the hallway.

Evan turned. Rolling up his sleeves, he leaned against the wall. Now, how did he tell his grandmother to butt out and stop being overly protective? This wasn't going to be easy.

"Evan, I don't like the way..." Donya hesitated. The look on Evan's face—-well, she wished he wouldn't scowl and glare at her. She worried about Maxi. The poor dear needed care and TLC.

Donya took a deep breath and moved toward Evan.

"I'm sorry." She shrugged and stopped short of having to crane her neck back to look at him. He wasn't a lanky teen. His life and practice were his own. He'd always be her fave grandson. Her only grandson. Ten simpering witch granddaughters were more than she could handle some days.

"Thank you, Abada. I get you want the best for Tia Maxi. The three of you are like sisters. But let me do what needs to be done for the physical ailments while you take care of the magical part. Okay?"

Donya smiled. She wanted to hug him like she did when he came up to her shoulders. Bear hugging a six-foot-tall male with her five feet three height wasn't easy. Instead, she patted his hand, slipped her arm around his waist, and squeezed. "Okay, but you need to understand that Maxi won't give up easily."

Evan squeezed back. "Abada, I don't expect her to. That's why I hope you got ahold of Aprell. She's the one other person Tia Maxi will listen to. I know she'll make sure Tia Maxi does what she's supposed to."

Donya nodded. "How about Tabby and I wait out here in the sitting area? I know you have other patients to see."

Evan reached down and cupped her cheek. She could see in his eyes his concern and worry. He didn't get that once a witch always a witch. He did the best he could. Maybe Aprell could help him understand. Perhaps Tabby was right. Aprell and Evan together might be a good idea.

"I love you, Abada. Let me take care of Tia Maxi's physical health, okay?" Evan patted her cheek. She smiled, rubbing her face against his hand.

"I get you," she said, stepping away from Evan. "I worry about you differently cuz. . ." Her voice trailed off. Why did his mortal status require extra concern and care? He wasn't a teen anymore, full of angst and curiosity. Could she change her innate nurturing to viewing him as the capable adult he was? It would take time and work. One she would undertake because of their blood bond and her love for him.

"Worry differently?" Evan quipped. "I think you aren't sure how to deal with a grown mortal."

Donya reached up, grabbing Evan's earlobe, tugging downward. "Don't underestimate me." She shook a finger at him, smiling as she continued speaking. "I might unspell that mirror in your bedroom."

Evan laughed as he leaned down, kissing her cheek. "If you do, I'm not responsible for the permanent blush you'll get."

"I yield that one to you. Send Tabby out. I'll be in the waiting area." Donya turned, smiling as she did. Even grown, Evan still enjoyed their banter. Ah, to be young again. Yes, time to find him a mate. Donya rolled her eyes heavenward as a shrill ring started deep in her left ear. A tiny grey speck appeared as the ringing grew. Taking a deep breath, she started humming.

"Granddad's song? He's communicating with you." Evan's chuckle sounded as Donya continued toward the waiting room door. "I bet he's got an ear full for you."

As she reached the door, Donya whispered. "Errol, a bit of match-making magic isn't going to hurt. Time Evan found..."

Enough! Helping him out is one thing. Love spelling someone isn't.

"Right. Crystal ball consulting and a couple of tarot readings will show us what we need to do." Donya pulled the door open, lowering the volume of her humming as she did. The ringing in her ears ceased with her first step into the waiting area. Ah ha! Errol kept an eye on Evan from the hereafter. Scold her, would he? Devious scamp still kept his pulse on everything. He dwelled on Evan as much as she did. Raising him after his parents died wasn't easy.

As Donya took a seat opposite the doorway, she looked out the window. Two commuter jets came into view making their descent into the local airport. Had Aprell made her flight?

CHAPTER THREE

Tabby wanted to stay with Maxi as Evan completed his examination of her. But Donya won out.

"Will you sit still?" Donya nudged her. "Evan will call us in as soon as he is done."

"Yes, but –"

Donya scowled at her. "No buts. Either we trust Evan, or we don't."

Tabby sighed and glanced around the nearly empty waiting room. A lone mother with her two small children sat across the room. Poor kids. Their tattered clothes and pale features said they needed help. Could they safely do it without using too much magic?

Tabby leaned to Donya. "Coven sister, that mother and children need our help. "

Donya snuck a glance at the mother. "I can tell from her proud carriage she doesn't want to ask for it. I know Evan donates his time to the free clinic down the block. They may be here for vaccinations."

"Can we help out with a bit of magic? Money in her wallet and a job?" Tabby unfolded her hands and began moving her fingers.

"Wait. Let me read her aura." Tabby watched as Donya began to close her eyes. She wouldn't completely close them. With her field of vision narrowed, focusing on the mother was her intent. Auras didn't lie. Most people didn't know how to shield.

Donya's breathing slowed. Tabby knew how to tell when she connected. Donya's own aura changed in brightness and showed more readily about her. Unless someone knew how to read them, no one understood why Donya flushed and her eyes appeared to glow. A few moments later, Donya flashed a smile and nodded.

"I know who needs help. Mrs. Tuttle down at the thrift store. She's been looking for full-time help." Tabby thrust her hand into her purse and felt different items until she found her small silver unicorn horn key ring and starburst crystal filled her hand. Inhaling slowly, Tabby partially closed her eyes and focused on the mother and children.

With each inhalation, she called upon her other coven sisters to link her telepathically to the cosmos and the powers-that-be to hear the need of those they sought to help. She heard Mrs. Tuttle's soft yes and two others of her coven added their offers of help. Tabby smiled as she released her charms. Materializing money was not a feat anyone tried. Too easy to be taken for counterfeit. Still the funds would be available to the family. Evan would help in delivering the message. He would balk some, but his heart knew she and Donya meant no harm. Besides, the poor dears needed a roof over their heads if the youngsters were to get over their illness.

Evan stepped into the hall. He opened his mouth ready to stop his grandmother. Rather than voice his thoughts, Evan cleared his throat and moved toward the mother and children.

"Hi, Lissa and Donovan. Feeling any better?" Evan squatted down so he was eye level with the children. He noted their paleness and red eyes. Tears again or more symptoms of their allergies taking affect. Bad enough, they were still getting over chest colds.

Lissa and Donovan nodded. Neither released their hold on their mother's arms. Evan wished he knew a way to help them. With good food, warm clothes, and a roof over their heads, the children would rebound. Their mother needed time to heal. Blast her stupid spouse and his thrill-seeking ways. Widowhood wasn't easy for anyone, but a young mother had double issues. How to care for her children and work possibly full time?

"Misty, my assistant will take Lissa and Donovan into the reception area to get their height and weights. We'll be able to see them from here. I have a couple of questions for your charts." Evan stood and motioned his assistant forward. He watched as she herded the children into the small alcove where they could still see their mother.

Evan pulled a chair up next to Misty. He wished she wasn't so skittish. She had every reason to be. Her stupid late husband had worked her over royally. Between the verbal and emotional abuse, it was no wonder she jumped every time Evan got near her. "Relax, please. I know you want the best for the twins. You need care, too. When did you last get a decent night's sleep and a meal?"

Donya watched Misty glance to her twins and back to Evan. Her fidgeting indicated her unease. Evan would get some information from her. Not all he needed. Bless him and his ability to access folks when they needed to speak up but refused to. This mother didn't want to ask for help. Donya made up her mind as Misty licked her lips for the second time.

"Misty, I'm Dr. Mitchell's grandmother. Maybe I can help you?" Donya offered her hand. If the young woman took it, Donya knew she'd be able to read her better. Donya rarely used this part of her magical gifts. Her clan head said many generations back, a group of druids married into the coven, enlarging their dwindling population. Many of their healing gifts and psychic abilities began showing up in the next generations.

Evan knew Abada was up to something. He'd learned to not judge before learning more as she worked her magic. Yet, there was something different in her movements and body language. She almost never called him Dr. Mitchell. He could sense the change in the energy around Misty as Abada moved closer. Her posture and nervous movement altered with each breath.

"Misty, my grandmother knows many people in the community." Evan wished Abada would stop putting words in his head. Damn, this telepathic link could be a pain at times.

"Complain later. Help is waiting for this family."

Evan was glad he'd learned not to flinch when Abada poured magic into him. Facing her, Evan motioned her forward. "Maybe you can explain better."

Donya smiled and stood next to Misty. "I know Mrs. Tuttle down at the thrift store. She's been looking for help for a while."

"I-I-I don't know." The tremor in Misty's voice cut deep into Donya. Fear iced its way down her back and into the pit of her stomach. Images of fists punching Misty and a harsh male voice cussing and degrading her flashed through Donya's third eye. No matter how long she lived, Donya didn't understand how anyone could turn on someone they professed to love. It made no sense. Of course, her coven swore by the Wiccan Creed. Harm ye none came through first and loudest. Though sometimes the harming ended up helping and the fine line between malicious and helpful blurred.

Donya reached out, thinking warmth and healing images as she did. Her hand touched Misty's arm. "I'm sure things are blurry right now. How about you try it out?"

"Th-the job?" Misty's hesitation and strong anxiety raced up Donya's arm, settling next to the fear, icing its way into her.

Donya inhaled, adding gold to her vision mixed with a burst of energy that spilled over the cold and leeriness wanting to take over. "Yes, dear. Mrs. Tuttle wants an onsite manager. There's an apartment over the store available, too."

Heat inched its way up to meet her palm. Good, the spell worked. Nothing more than a suggestion along with a subtle flux of energy directed toward the outer shell the poor dear wore. Unsure and fragile came to mind. Yet a stark flash came through as Misty's gaze met hers. A man lay on the floor holding his hand to his face. The image grew and cleared more. It was as if she saw through Misty's eyes. A set of nunchucks dangled from her hand. Surprise had its merits.

"Ye-yes," Misty replied, nodding. "I got him. We ran."

Donya looked back at Evan. His wide-eyed look told her he didn't know a lot about his patient. Moving forward, he spoke. "You're safe now. He can't follow. We'll make sure of that."

"How?" Misty stood a bit straighter, reaching out toward her children.

"You're prayers got an answer." Donya patted Misty's arm. "Some things you just know."

Evan coughed, cleared his throat and spoke. "Misty, Mrs. Tuttle and my grandmother go way back. You know Police Chief Dan Chernoff."

Misty nodded.

"He's Mrs. Tuttle's grandson." Evan laid his hand on Donya's shoulder. "You're safe."

"As I can be for now," Misty added without stuttering.

"Yes, dear. That is so true for any of us." Donya smiled, stepping back until she was next to Evan. "Shall I tell Mrs. Tuttle. . ."

She let her words trail off, waiting to see if Misty answered.

"Tell her I'm interested," Misty spoke clearer and firmer.

"Good. Leave your number with Evan. I'll have Mrs. Tuttle contact him." Donya turned, made her way with Tabby following across the waiting room and sat down.

"Abada," Evan began, crossing to where she sat. "Tia Maxi will be out shortly."

"Thank you, Evan." Donya leaned over and kissed his cheek as he bent down.

"Thank you for helping Misty. She deserves a break." Evan hugged her and stood up.

"You're welcome. Comes with being a responsible witch." Donya grinned as Evan shook his head. "Go attend to your patient."

Evan took Misty and her children with him leaving a few patients remaining in the waiting room. Most of them nodded each time Donya looked up from the magazine she leafed through. Tabby played solitaire on her cell phone.

Ten minutes passed before Evan's assistant, holding a manila folder, opened the door. Tabby could make out the white slip the assistant's thumb held on top of the folder. Maxi's frown as she entered the waiting room said more than if she spoke. News wasn't what she expected.

Maxi made her way across the waiting room and sat down between Donya and Tabby. She glanced at both of them, leaned back and heaved a deep sigh. "Could either of you talk to Evan and. . ." She looked at both her coven sisters again, slumping down deeper.

Donya cupped her good hand between hers. "Maxi, Evan takes care of your physical health. What he prescribes must be necessary."

Tabby leaned against her, nodding as she spoke. "I'm starved. How about lunch at the Relief Society's cafeteria? We can talk more there."

Maxi stuck out her tongue. She didn't care how juvenile she appeared. Talk about the Relief Society Home came up too much during Evan's discussion with her. He'd dropped Aprell's name more than once. Calling her granddaughter was bad enough. Betwixting star! She wasn't addled or casting weird spells. So she missed her mark occasionally—Mr. Yost had thanked her for showing interest in his grandson. She'd gotten a lunch date out of it. Blasted cast would slow her down and that lunch date would have to wait. But moving out of her home, in with a bunch of bumbling, inept male and female witches made her sound and feel very old. Two hundred wasn't over the hill. Just slightly over the rise.

"Let's try something different," Donya suggested. "The new Mexican place down the street."

"Ooh, yes," Maxi said, sitting up. "Jalapeño Cheese Poppers with three alarm salsa! Yummy!"

Donya held up her hand. "Lunch, dear. Not a fire-spitting contest to see who can set off their sprinkler system."

Tabby rose, slinging her purse over her shoulder. "None of us needs indigestion half the night either. I'm up for some guacamole and chips along with one of their po'boy sandwiches."

"The one with shrimp tossed in jambalaya seasoning, along with beans and rice with a peach mango dressing?" Maxi struggled to stand up. Tabby held out her hand. Maxi took it and looked at Donya.

"Yes, that's the one I heard about from the librarian when I dropped off the boxes of books Mrs. Tuttle donated for the book sale." Donya picked up Maxi's purse. Put it over her shoulder with hers and held out both hands. She bent her knees slightly. "Ready when you are."

Maxi snorted, giggled and grabbed her arm. "On three."

"One," Tabby said.

"Two," Maxi said.

"Three," Donya added, gripping Maxi's forearm with her free hand.

A few groans followed by cuss words in every foreign language they knew filled the air as they moved back and forth until Maxi stood up. Donya let go, put both hands in the small of her back and stretched.

Tabby glanced around the waiting room. Everyone appeared interested in the magazine or newspaper they held up, not in three old women grunting and cussing. She glanced over her shoulder. Evan stood in the entry to the hall leading back to the examination rooms. A thousand-watt smile lit up his eyes and face. She shrugged. He nodded. Waited until Donya turned around and snickered.

"Abada, do you need a pain meds script? Sounds like you could use it." Evan walked toward them. Tabby rolled her eyes as Maxi glanced at her. Donya was busy shaking her finger at Evan.

'Keep it up, and I'll—-" Donya stopped as a newspaper rustled close to her. She grinned, waved at the person and said. "Evan, I'll be on my way. Thank you for the offer."

Evan met her at the exit to his office. He hugged her, kissed her cheek and handed her four pieces of paper. "Maxi's scripts, a referral to Dr. Kwang for acupuncture and a referral to Dr. Maxwell."

"Kenneth Maxwell, you went to med school with?" Donya asked, taking the scripts and referral forms.

"Yes. He moved to town a few months ago. He wanted a fresh start." Evan leaned closer and whispered. "Post-divorce. No matchmaking spells, okay?"

Donya pointed at herself. "Me? I don't matchmake. I illuminate those that need a match." She narrowed her eyes and stared at Evan.

Evan held up a hand, saying. "Not me either, Abada."

Donya grinned, widened her eyes, and said. "I yield."

Evan hugged her again and held the door as she, Tabby and Maxi exited.

Halfway to the elevator, Tabby asked, "You do know the waiting room overheard most of your conversation?"

Donya laughed. "Yes and most of them know that we witches are honor-bound."

"Good because the aura Evan's receptionist gives off every time he's around is hot enough to boil water."

Donya nodded as she pushed the elevator call button. "You can't miss her thoughts. She wants him bad. However, the want is purely hormonal. She's looking for someone who wants to add to the two kids she already has."

"Her best option is the male nurse she's been dating. He took care of me at the emergency room. He asked if she still worked for Evan," Maxi added, entering the elevator.

Tabby sighed. "You'd think we were the local matchmakers the way everyone asks us about who is with who."

Donya laughed, joining Tabby and Maxi in the elevator. "We just happen to frequent the places where a lot of singles are. Like the hospital, community events, and the Relief Society luncheons."

"I'm not frequenting those!" Maxi vehemently spit out. "Mr. Yost asked me out. I got a fella."

Tabby patted Maxi's shoulder. "Dear, it takes more than an offer to say you got a fella."

Maxi opened her mouth to retort. Donya stepped between Tabby and Maxi, holding up a hand. "You're on restriction until that arm heals. You know that."

"Yes. You called Aprell and told her I needed a keeper."

"You overheard?"

"Yes. I can't do anything about it now. She's on her way."

Tabby looked at her watch. "Yes, she left late evening Hawaii time. She should be in Nashville in an hour."

CHAPTER FOUR

Nashville International Airport

Aprell watched the luggage conveyor belt start. There was no mistaking her bright rainbow-colored suitcase. Neon stood out, and very few would mistakenly snag the case as theirs. The monogrammed strap surrounding the case set it apart as well. The Gothic letters were a pain to stitch. Yet, in the end, she knew her time and effort brought her satisfaction and a sense of joy. Joy, she'd accomplished a monotonous task. One that took concentration and focus. Like the challenge before her now. Helping her proud, independent grandmother accept she'd changed. A bell sounded, and the first pieces of luggage slid onto the conveyor belt. Several more followed until her case made the slide down and a loop around to where she stood. She attached her tote to the case's strap, clicked it closed, pulled up the handle and exited the luggage claim area. A few feet away, she found the concierge's desk.

"I need to get to Sylvan Valley." She glanced at the shuttle schedule trying to determine which one she needed.

"The next shuttle leaves in two hours." The clerk started entering her info into the computer.

"I can get you there faster," a vaguely familiar voice said.

Aprell blinked, scowled, took a breath and put on her best smile as she turned, ready to say no. Her throat went dry. Words failed her. Her mouth opened and closed like a fish gasping for water. He'd gotten leaner, toned and still had that dang silly grin. Evan hadn't changed, and yet he had.

"Uhm," she began. "How did you know?"

Evan chuckled. " Tia Maxi gave me last year's Christmas photo." He held out the photo. "Nice tan."

Aprell reached for the photo. "Yes. Thanks."

Evan pulled the photo back. "No. Promised to return it." He slid it into his jacket pocket.

Aprell turned to the clerk. "Thank you. I've got my ride."

Evan reached for her suitcase. "I can do that." She grabbed the handle, yanking the case to her.

"Your choice." Evan turned and started walking away.

Aprell slung her purse over her shoulder and dragged the case with her. She'd forgotten how fast Evan could walk and clear distances. "Hey," she called out, picking up her pace. "Slow down. *Please.*"

Evan halted, turned and watched Aprell trot toward him. Okay, he'd given into a jolt of teenage memories and Abada's reminder to be a gentleman. Lord, what a way to yank him out of doctor mode and into the here and now. Instead of his usual patient and symptom concentration, he could shift into off-duty mode. He never completely got into not being a doctor. Saving lives mattered. Caring mattered. Being mattered. He moved toward Aprell. "Sorry. Habit. My assistant calls me on it, too."

Aprell nodded. "Comes with the job. Doctors focus on their patients."

Evan waited until she reached him to reply. "You get it? Why I choose to practice in Sylvan Valley and not somewhere else?"

Aprell grinned. "Yup. My practice takes me places I hadn't expected to find dedicated doctors."

"Your practice?" he asked turning, surveying the crowd.

"Yes. I'll explain later." Aprell pointed toward the closest exit. "Through there?"

"Actually, I'm in the close-in parking lot." He glanced at his watch. "I paid for an hour. We got forty minutes. Wanna grab some coffee?"

Aprell shook her head. "No thanks. I had two cups on the plane. I don't need the jitters."

"I know that feeling. Decaf is all I drink. Let's grab a couple bottles of water and head to the car." He pointed to the snack shop close to the exit near them. "Might want to grab a snack."

Ten minutes later, Aprell trailed Evan toward the door. She knew she couldn't keep up with him if he didn't slow down. "Evan," she called out, trying to get around a group of loud, noisy teens standing near the exit. "Slow down. I can't keep up."

Evan paused, turned and held up his hand. He made his way around the teens and met her. "Sorry. Bad habit I have."

"Not really. I was right behind you until people cut in front of me or stopped." Aprell shoved the handle of her case down, unhooked her tote from the carry strap, and faced Evan. "Do you mind carrying this?"

Evan turned the case on its side and picked it up by the handle. "No problem. Hold my hand, and we'll get out of here."

Aprell wiped her sweat-slick palm on her skirt and put her hand in his. Heat shot across her palm, sizzling up and down her arm before settling deep in her stomach. She shook her head, glancing at Evan who kept looking straight ahead like nothing happened. He hadn't felt it? She knew from reading auras and working with her crystals that intense heat wasn't elusive. It left its mark even without searing or burning. "What kind of car are you driving now?"

Evan glanced at her, stepping into the lane of traffic whizzing up and down the arrival and departure lanes. He tightened his grip on her hand. More heat oozed off him and into her. Countering the effects took concentration even for the brief block spell to take effect. *Heat and desire stay...*

A horn honked. "Watch out," Evan called out, tugging her to him.

Aprell stumbled, her purse and tote slid down her shoulder. "Easier said than done. Damn, no one is paying attention to what they're doing."

Evan scooted between stopped cars, almost dragging her along with him. "Attention is on getting into the next space or lane while they gawk at their phone."

"That's for sure," Aprell yelled as another car zoomed past them, honking its horn.

The game of cat and mouse dodging cars continued with a few quick stops until they stepped onto the opposite sidewalk. "Damn," Evan said, shaking his head. "Talk about accidents waiting to happen."

"Yes. And we were in the crosswalk, too!" Aprell moved to the stairs leading into the garage. "Your car a secret or you gonna tell me what you're driving?"

Evan laughed. "No secret. The same red sports car I bought last year of my residency."

"The odometer must have turned over twice."

Evan started down the stairs. "No. Just close to a hundred thousand. Living close to work helps keep the mileage down."

"Walking helps keep you and your car healthy." Aprell trotted past Evan and stopped three steps down.

"Except in snow and ice. Car is important then." Evan pointed to his left. "Third parking spot past the door."

Aprell nodded and entered the garage. Third spot on the left sat the red two-door sports car with a license plate that read *MD @ HART.* As she turned back toward Evan, a beep sounded, and the trunk hatch opened.

"Easy access, especially when you're running late." Evan chuckled. "Not that I do that much."

Aprell snickered. "Just like you did in high school?"

"Hey, I resemble that remark," he bantered back.

"Yes, you do. I seem to remember a few of our teachers claimed we were twins due to the late thing." Aprell took her suitcase from Evan and put it in the trunk.

"Can't help we had to carpool together." Evan opened the passenger door for her. "Even then our families thought we needed brought together."

Aprell sighed as she fastened her seatbelt and set her tote and purse on the floor between her feet. Tia Donya or her grandmother tried matchmaking her and Evan more than once. Each time it blew up in a large caldron of smoke and bitter angst. They'd bickered and fought like siblings instead of friends which they worked out on their own. Sure, she'd asked Evan to prom, and he took her to homecoming, but that didn't make them a couple or ready to instantaneously fall in love. They'd dated on the sly for a couple of months until someone outed them and told their families. So much for letting them decide on their own if they became a couple.

Evan walked around the car. He knew that sigh as if he'd heard it many times. The sigh of frustration and meddling loving families. That was one of the reasons why he'd gone to med school in New York. Distance and time permitted him to find himself. Find through trial and error who he was without worrying about another magic taunting him or the 'poor you' looks and advice no one got. Magics didn't understand not being magical, and mortals didn't get being magical. It had taken Abada a while to understand his frustration and request she let him find things out on his own. Trial and error had its advantages once Abada agreed with him on his approach, she backed him almost one hundred percent. Excepting her to see things entirely from a mortal side wasn't realistic and he had to compromise when it came to his trying to see things from a magic side. Life experience and abilities varied from person to person, species to species.

"Okay," Evan said, starting the car. "We're in this together. Not because someone decided for us. We made the choice out of love. Love for our families."

"True," Aprell replied as they pulled out of the garage. "Love knows no barriers and boundaries. It exists in most life forms."

"Yep," he said, merging into traffic. "That's one thing magics and mortals agree upon."

Twenty minutes passed before Evan spoke again. "You know why you're here."

"My grandmother."

"Yes. I'm sorry it took this to get you here." He glanced in the rearview mirror. The exit to the rest area was coming up. He wanted a neutral place to talk about Tia Maxi and his suspicions. Abada and Tia Tabby had slowed down on their own. They hadn't stopped being active. They'd changed interest and how they practiced magic. Tia Maxi wasn't slowing down. She'd taken on more with buying the apartment complex, tutoring young magics, and spell casting complex magic. Couldn't she understand with age came the opportunity to not have to be all things?

"Why do you say that?"

"I know you come to visit once a year. Maybe twice. Most of the time, I'm on vacation or attending continuing ed conferences."

"Nothing gets by our grandmothers."

Evan snorted as he changed lanes. "Something I accepted a while back is we're each other's extended family."

"No denying that. I think we've heard or shared most major events growing up."

"Sure did. I want to talk about Tia Maxi without Abada and Tia Tabby around." Evan parked the car.

Aprell unfastened her seatbelt and faced him. "It's that bad?"

Evan opened his door, pointing to a table not far from the car. "Depends on your definition of bad. Let's sit at the table over there and snack while we talk."

Aprell nodded, got out of the car and quietly walked over to the table. She faced him as she straddled the table's bench. Worry etched her face like ice frosting a window. There was no mistaking her concern. Not that he wanted to. Tia Maxi needed care and assistance that living alone didn't provide.

Evan set his bag on the table and sat on the bench across from Aprell before he spoke again. He laid his hand on the table palm up, cleared his throat and said, "What did Abada and Tia Tabby tell you?"

"Grandmother fell, hurt her arm and legs trying to skateboard." Aprell shook her head. She opened her water bottle and drank. Recapping it, she set it on the table. "I suspect I didn't get the whole story."

Evan bit into his apple. Juice ran down his chin, dripping onto his jacket and shirt. He reached for a napkin as Aprell's hand grazed his. Sparks! Two bright sparks flashed before him. What the hell? Had someone bespelled something of his? Or was Aprell more magical than she'd let on in the past?

"You're right." Evan waited until Aprell's gaze met his. "Tia Maxi's got two hairline fractures along with a badly bruised wrist. Then there's her legs."

"Crap," Aprell groaned. "Doesn't sound good."

Evan nodded. He drank part of his water. "She's in a cast. I got her referrals to an orthopedic surgeon friend and to an acupuncturist I know. Sorry I'm the one breaking the news."

Aprell looked at him, blinked and glanced away. She tore open her bag of trail mix, popping two pieces of chocolate out of it into her mouth. He watched her chest rise and fall with each breath she took. Her full breasts caught his attention momentarily, and he looked away. Lusting after one of your grandmother's best friend's daughter wasn't a good idea. At least not at the moment. Evan opened his mouth to speak when Aprell held her hand—palm up toward him—away from her.

"I'm not mad at you. Grandmother needs to slow down. She isn't a young witch."

"I agree. She doesn't want to move to the Relief Society Home to quote her, 'It's for washed up witches and mages.'"

Aprell ate more of her trail mix, drank some water and let go a deep sigh. "Suggestions? Your prognosis?"

"Long term, if Tia Maxi follows the orthopedist's instructions and does her physical therapy, she'll regain full use of her arm and wrist. Hairline fractures can turn into full-blown breaks if she isn't careful."

"She can be hardheaded and stubborn." Aprell finished her trail mix and water.

"We all can. That's why I gave her referrals to Dr. Maxwell and Dr. Kwang." Evan took two last bites of his apple, chewed, and swallowed. "That's part of the reason I told Abada and Tia Tabby to call you."

Aprell nodded. "Dr. Maxwell? Kenneth Maxwell, we went to school with?"

"One in the same. He moved back a couple months ago."

"You referred grandmother to him because?" Aprell capped her bottle.

Evan turned sideways, straddling the bench. "He's a good orthopedist. And he's one of them."

"One of them?"

Evan nodded, looking away. "Yes, one of them. A magic. I'm sure Tia Maxi wants one of her kind taking care of her."

Aprell licked her lips, pressed them together and inhaled. That part hadn't changed. Evan's tone wasn't flat like it used to be when he made similar declarations. There was some warmth to his pitch, but why hadn't he looked at her. Retorts, questions and yes, accusations filled her mind and mouth. She couldn't say them, even give them credence. Apparently, Evan still felt like an outsider. Shunned because he wasn't magical. One question wouldn't go away. It kept popping up, clamoring for attention. Her curiosity wanted to know.

Folding her hands together, she asked the question. "Why?"

Evan laid both hands on the table, faced her and said. "Cause Tia Maxi's twitching isn't working."

"She's lost her magic?"

"Not completely."

"I don't get it. I want you to try to explain." Aprell stuffed her empty bottle in the plastic bag laying on the table.

Evan stared at her, rolled his eyes, and shrugged. "I can only tell you what I've heard and know."

"Go for it." Aprell reached across the table for Evan's empty bottle. "I appreciate you sharing what you can."

"She stops mid-spells like she's forgotten the words. Her sleight of hand isn't working either. She drops things, fumbles with magic items, and a few are complaining her love potions backfired." Evan stood. "She balks at any mention of the Relief Society."

Aprell picked up her purse and the plastic bag holding their trash. "Thank you. I know you're limited on what you can tell me."

Evan held out his hand as he rounded the table. "I'm concerned about Tia Maxi. She, Tia Tabby and you are parts of my extended family by choice. I want the best for her."

Aprell started to walk away from the table. Evan moved up beside her. She held out the bag of trash. He shook his head, took hold of her empty hand and squeezed it. He turned and stepped away from her, not letting go of her hand or loosening his grip. She glanced at their hands and inhaled sharply. Red lines laced their way around their hands and wrists. Other times she'd seen this . . .no it couldn't be. Someone's match-making attempt had to have backfired again. Yes, that had to be it. Couldn't they leave well enough alone?

CHAPTER FIVE

Aprell glanced at Evan. He hadn't said anything since they'd left the rest stop. Time wasn't their enemy. At least their discussion wasn't heated. Nor had either of them lost their composure. She'd tried to pick up where their discussion had left off twice in the last thirty minutes. He'd held up his hand and didn't offer why he wouldn't say more. Leaning back into her seat, she let go a silent sigh and focused on the view out the passenger window.

Evan wet his lips, gripping the steering wheel tighter. Twice he'd come close to blurting out his thoughts, pulling his hand away from Aprell's. Static electricity didn't leave a shock that kept on repeating even after its initial zap. Not like what had jigged its path along his wrist and up his arm and jolted his psyche in a way that hadn't happened in quite a while. He inhaled and slowly exhaled, wondering what to say. How did you tell someone—Abada's best friend's daughter—you wanted to spend a few hours blissing you both out sexually? Likely to get him punched, yelled at and spells tossed at him just from Aprell. Deity only knew what Abada and Tia Maxi would do and say. Refusing to talk wasn't getting them anywhere. He'd gotten Tia Maxi the best mortal medical help he could. She might listen to her coven sisters and magical cohorts better than he and his geriatric counterparts.

"I'm sorry I blew you off earlier. I've been racking my brain how to help Tia Maxi more." He glanced at Aprell as he merged into traffic to exit the main highway and continue east toward Sylvan Valley.

"Why didn't you say so?" Aprell turned slightly toward him. "You know reading minds isn't one of my magics."

Evan pressed his lips firmly together. He counted to ten in a mix of French, Spanish and Latin, and once in English. The retort burning his throat, ready to spill out his mouth, died as he reached ten again. Goddess above, they weren't seventeen. They'd matured, moved beyond two prickly porcupines tossing quills at each other. Well, they had, hadn't they? He shook his head as he pulled into the right lane and slowed down to the posted speed limit. "I wouldn't know what your magics are. I ain't got none, remember?"

Aprell stuck her tongue out at him. Last time she'd done that he'd grabbed her, French kissed her and ended up with a bruised shin and sore pecks on one arm. He'd do it again if she weren't...weren't what? Baiting him? At ease with him? Or so attracted to him? *Fuck that idea!* his psyche crowed, loud and vigorously. *It's you who's attracted.* Evan took another deep breath, exhaled and shoved his noisy, obnoxious conscience to the back of his mind. Not that did much good 'cuz later it would catch him off-guard and wallop him with its imaginative two-by-four. Been there, done that, and had no wish to experience that again.

"Your cuteness with that antic ended our junior year, remember?" There, he'd changed the tactic. Sent it back her direction. A dumb move he'd done repeatedly during high school. Could he move beyond the old feelings and images Aprell ignited in him?

Aprell flexed her hands, clenched them tight and arched her shoulders like she was stretching. She was with other aspects added in. Stretching her patience, her desire to retort and push Evan's buttons like she used to. In junior high and high school. . .Ten years plus removed, neither of them had changed? Or was this a sparring match to see who came out on top? "I remember."

She glanced at Evan again, flexed her hands and shoved them under her legs. She wasn't going to start waving them around and get loud. Nothing came from that except more angst and louder discussions. The topic wasn't one that needed defending. She rolled her shoulders again, put her hands in her lap and said, "I apologize."

Evan glanced at her, nodded, and looked away. "I do."

"Thanks," she began. "I need to shift my thinking to include non-magic views."

"Thanks. That'll help. I gotta shift mine. Most of my patients are mortal."

"I work with a lot of mortals. Dr. Haupt sends magics and mortals to me."

"Sounds interesting. I'd like to focus on Tia Maxi for now. Okay?"

Aprell nodded and glanced at her watch. Ninety minutes until they reached Sylvan Valley. Keeping the conversation on her grandmother took focus. Focus each of them needed. "Sure," Aprell said, slouching in the seat. "Our grandmothers aren't handling aging well."

Evan chuckled. "Some days they are. Others, you're so right."

"What is grandmother doing that has you worried most?" Her short call from Tia Donya and Tia Tabby gave her the basics. Her grandmother had hurt herself, her magic misfired often, and she needed a caregiver. Some of it Aprell got. Evan had filled in more. Not enough to give her a thorough understanding.

"Tia Maxi's breaks need time to heal. She's overly stubborn when it comes to admitting she needs help."

"Tia Donya said Grandmother fussed every time they mentioned the Relief Society. I get she's got physical bruises and trauma you're working on. How can I help?"

Evan pulled the car onto the shoulder, turned on the flashers and faced her. "Keep an eye on her. Get her to her appointments. Help her realize none of us wants to take away her independence."

"Tall orders," Aprell replied. "She's been on her own since she and granddad divorced."

"Decades ago, I know." Evan shook his head. "She's got to think twice about magic too. Abada says single-mindedness is what keeps her on target."

"I'll do what I can. Let me think on this and come up with some ideas." Aprell yawned. "Sorry, I need a nap. Sleeping on the plane isn't the same as in your own bed."

Evan turned off the flashers and eased onto the highway. "Nap away. How long you want?"

"Forty-five minutes. I do my best thinking when I meditate which gets me to sleep." Aprell reclined her seat some and straightened her skirt. She reached out, touched Evan's arm and added. "Thank you. You're doing a great job with Grandmother. Sometimes hearing a thank you is important."

"You're right," Evan responded, turning on the wipers as large raindrops spattered against the windshield. "It's going to take us both to give and get Tia Maxi the best care. Aprell, I'm glad you're back."

Aprell blinked, pressed her lips together, and kept her thoughts to herself. Evan was right; it would take both of them to get her grandmother what she needed. *He was glad she was back?* Her experience said don't believe him. Ten years could change a person. She'd seen bits and pieces of this already. Time to examine this could come later. Concentrating on how she could team up with Evan otherwise took priority.

Aprell closed her eyes, inhaled and exhaled slowly, allowing the hum of the car speeding along the highway to lull her into a space between awake and entering light sleep.

Maxi handed the server her menu. She picked up her napkin, shook it out and laid it on her lap. One-handed eating and doing with her right hand wasn't easy. She'd found that out the hard way trying to fasten her bra this morning. Laying her casted arm on the table, she sighed. "Soup and taquitos isn't much of a lunch. I want cheese jalapeño poppers."

Donya reached across the table, laying her hand on the cast. "How about an order to go? Fifteen of them as a meal might be more than your stomach can handle."

"Aprell deserves one night to get used to the time change without dealing with your indigestion." Tabby drank some of her water. "How you eat those things is beyond me."

"I pick them up, smother them with salsa, and pop em in my mouth. Then I chew 'em up." Maxi glared at Tabby. "Not even a margarita with lunch?"

"What did the pharmacist say?" Donya reached for the white pharmacy bag sitting toward the back of the table.

"No alcohol, no spicy food, and lots of yogurt. Bleck. I hate bland food!" Maxi grabbed the bag and tossed it at Donya. "I hate being sick."

Donya raised her hand, pointed at the bag and spoke. "Land on the table. Now."

The bag floated to the table, settling close to her. She pushed the bag aside and leaned forward. "Maxi, I get you're frustrated. Don't take it out on Tabby and me."

Maxi slumped down in the booth. "Sorry. I'm hungry. And anxious."

"Anxious about what?" Tabby asked.

"Aprell and what the other doctors are going to say." Maxi drank some of her water and nibbled on a peperjack cheese bread stick. She chewed and swallowed. "I'm not useless."

Donya nodded. She knew that feeling well. Evan had said the same thing when two of his childhood best friends ostracized him due to his magicless state. Getting someone to see their worth other ways took patience and time. "No, dear you're not. Limited, yes. Useless, no."

"I agree," Tabby added. "Why do you think you're useless?"

"My magic sucks. You said so. Both of you. So what am I good for?" Maxi waved her breadstick in the air. "A witch without magic is like giving a pig wings. We don't know what to do."

Donya pressed her lips tightly together. Maxi's sense of humor came through loud and clear along with her sarcasm. Limitations mixed with changes presented challenges. Ones that some faced with zeal. Others with dread and depression. Maxi thought she was washed up-over and done to use a once popular cliché. One every witch faced until she learned a new skill or different view. Donya wet her lips and spoke. "Not useless. New witches need training. We can help out there. Honing our remaining skills takes time and study."

"Lots of practice. The Relief Society believes in that. Encourages it." Tabby added.

"Like newbie magics learning how to control and spell cast all over again." Maxi sighed and slumped deeper in her seat.

"Isn't what we do every day practice?" Donya asked. "Practice living, doing and being better than we were the day before. I don't mind practice. Perfect and excellent might be boring and stagnant."

Tabby chuckled. "I hear some of the elders like teaching and learning from the newbies. Some have added new tricks and talent."

Maxi tossed her breadstick on the table. "I'm not washed up. I've got value."

"None of us are," Donya countered. "I suspect you're hangry as Evan often says."

"Hangry?" Maxi asked, repeating the word a couple more times.

"Yes," Donya replied. "A mix of hungry and angry. Hangry."

"See. You learned a new word. Not so bad," Tabby added.

Maxi picked up her bread stick and put it on the plate in front of her, nodding at the same time. "Okay. One word doesn't change everything."

"Ladies, sorry for the delay on your order. Soup and taquitos with a side of mango salsa. Chef Mario saw you come in. He sent this out special for you, Miss Maxi." The server set the order in front of Maxi.

"Thank you," Maxi replied, picking up one of the taquitos, dipping it in the salsa and biting into it. She chewed and swallowed while the server set Tabby and Donya's food in front of them.

"Thank Chef Mario for me. This salsa is sweet with a small kick." Maxi dipped the rest of her taquito into the salsa.

Donya picked up her knife and fork. "Enjoy, my friend. I'm glad this won't give you heartburn later."

Tabby nodded, biting into her po'boy sandwich.

Twenty minutes passed as they ate in silence. Maxi laid her soupspoon on the table and wiped her mouth with her napkin. She belched, grinned and picked up her water glass. "Here's to good food, good friends and fried ice cream."

Donya laughed. "I think I saw flavor of the day is Dulce Leche."

Tabby pushed her plate away from her. "Oh, my stomach make room for some of that." She raised her water glass, clicked it against Maxi's and drank.

Donya scooted to the end of the booth seat, rose and picked up her purse. "I see our server back by the bar near the restroom. I'll send her over."

Making her way across the dining area, Donya signaled to their server. She came over. She smiled as Donya told her what they wanted. The server nodded and started toward the table. Donya continued on to the restroom. Maxi didn't need to worry about cooking tonight. Mario would make sure dinner arrived hot and ready for Aprell and her.

Ten minutes later as Donya exited the restroom, their server greeted her. "Chef Mario says call when you're ready for the food to be delivered."

"Thank you. And our check?" Donya asked.

"Ready after you all enjoy your dessert, compliments of Chef Mario." The server stepped away into the kitchen area directly behind the bar.

Donya sat back down, glancing at Tabby who grinned and winked. Maxi smiled. "What have you two been up to?"

"Oh, a bit of matchmaking for ourselves." Maxi pointed at the salted margarita glass near her. "Virgin margarita. I'm behaving."

Donya smiled, shook her head and replied. "Depends on your definition of behaving."

Tabby chortled. "With me chaperoning her, you bet she's behaving."

Donya glanced over her shoulder. Their server approached again carrying a tray with steaming coffee mugs and their desserts. "I see you managed to get our desserts free of charge, Tabby."

Tabby ducked her head as Donya looked at her. "Mario came out and asked Maxi about her arm."

"Yes, after he asked you out to the Saturday night Relief Society social." Maxi picked up her spoon. "I hope he remembered the extra chocolate sauce I asked for."

Sips of coffee and bites of dessert filled the next several moments as each savored the strong chicory coffee laced with honey and cream mixing with the caramel sweet ice cream.

Maxi looked up as she laid her spoon down. Tabby kept glancing back toward the bar and grinning. Donya was looking at her cell phone. Twice she'd picked it up, shook her head as she viewed it, and laid it on the table. They had things to keep them busy. People and tasks, hobbies and interests and . . .she had tenants, a granddaughter who lived cross country and loneliness to occupy her. What a bunch of nothing. Books on tape, books from the library and the occasional flirt with her neighbor across the street filled the nooks and crannies of the endless silence and boredom she loathed. When had she lost touch with being active, teaching younger witches and mages about magical responsibility or even sharing a meal with a group of friends beyond Donya and Tabby? Maybe the Relief Society wasn't such a bad idea after all. She'd have more of her friends around her and . . .

"Maxi, I know that look." Donya laid her hand on hers. "You don't have to give up."

Maxi curled her lips in her best fake smile and shook her head. "No, I don't. Maybe it's time for change."

"Change?" Tabby asked, arching an eyebrow as she reached for the check the server had put face down on the table. "What kind of change are you talking about?"

"Embracing the Relief Society. I shouldn't be alone. I should slow down. Accept I'm old. My magic is. . ."

"*Enough*!" Donya demanded. She leaned forward, pointing at Maxi with her cell phone. "This isn't about shoulds and shouldn'ts. Or washed up or old useless mentality."

"Then what's it about?" Maxi laid her wallet on the table.

"Acceptance. Self-acceptance. Knowing you're worth living and being. And—" Donya looked at Tabby, nudging her.

"What?" Tabby looked up from the bill. Donya nodded toward Maxi. "Oh, yes. And helping others. Reaching out to the community and lending a hand. We're helping Misty land a job with Mrs. Tuttle."

"Probably using magic," Maxi suggested, pulling a twenty out of her wallet and laying it on the table. "Isn't that against our coven's creed? Even the Wiccan Rede?"

"Helping is talking about the job. Encouraging Misty to go for an interview. And yes, magic is in there." Tabby picked up Maxi's twenty and laid it with her ten and five. She pushed the bill toward Donya.

Donya held up her hand. "Before you start spouting more creeds and oaths at us. We sent healing magic out to all in Evan's waiting room. Even his assistant Ellen. She's unsure about a lot."

"How do you know?" Maxi asked, setting her purse on the table.

"Her aura screams it. Just like Misty's did. Like yours has. Even Tabby's on occasion. A bit of prayer, reiki encouragement and a positive spell is all I did."

Tabby nodded. "I sent energy with her. Misty made her own decision. We connected via the coven's psychic link with Mrs. Tuttle to let her know."

"So what about Aprell and Evan?" Maxi scooted to the edge of the booth and slung her purse onto her good shoulder.

"What about them?" Donya asked, adding her twenty to the pile of money. She picked the check and cash up and rose.

Tabby exited the booth, picked up her purse and faced Maxi. "It's not like we're matchmaking them."

Maxi faced Donya, giving her a slow once-overlook with both eyebrows arched as she squinted. She turned and faced Tabby, giving her the same lingering stare and frowning glare. Maxi inhaled, shook her head and said, "Bull shit. I ain't buying it, sisters."

CHAPTER SIX

Maxi squeezed between Donya and Tabby, not looking back. She didn't believe they weren't hoping Aprell and Evan got together. They'd tossed magic at both of them previously. Maxi paused close to the front door, glancing over her shoulder. Tabby and Donya were talking with their server, who kept shaking her head. Leaving large cash tips threw many wait staff off guard. They worked hard for the tips and wages they got. Maxi smiled as Donya pressed the cash into their server's hand, nodding and saying something. She didn't need to read Donya's lips to know what she said. The woman had earned the tip and would split with the busboy who approached the table. The amount would be split between them equally without either feeling cheated or left out.

Maxi inhaled deeply and let go a matching sigh. It wasn't her norm to give up. She felt like it at times. Spells gone awry. Mixed up incantations and wrong ingredients in potions. That racked up several points on her negativity meter. Her biggest downer was having Aprell come help. Aprell had worked hard to get her business up and running. Finding a place she felt comfortable in and at home had ranked high for her. She hadn't let on when she moved cross-country. Maxi shook her head. Aprell's actions and unspoken message came through loud and clear. Get away from Sylvan Valley and Evan. As far away as she could.

"Shaking your head isn't going to change a thing," Donya teased, coming up behind her.

"No, it doesn't. Pushing my emotions down doesn't work either." Maxi faced Donya. "Expressing them and feeling them is important."

"I agree," Tabby added, moving past them. She pulled on her sweater, adding, "It's a warm, sunny afternoon. Let's walk down to the park."

Maxi tugged her sweater out of her purse and worked it over her cast. "A walk sounds wonderful. Evan suggested I get out and walk to help ease the stiffness in my legs."

Donya helped her get her arm in the other sleeve of her sweater. Donya took her ruana out of her purse and slipped it over her head. "Down to the park and back. Good idea. We'll get the car on the way back."

Maxi nodded as she slid past Tabby who held the door open. Outside, she faced Donya and Tabby. "We haven't heard from Evan or Aprell. I hope they're getting along."

Donya snorted. "I think they can work their own tiffs out. They're past babysitting age."

Tabby chuckled as she moved up beside Donya. Maxi grasped the straps of her purse tighter and pointed toward the park ten blocks away. "Sometimes you got to let go and let them figure it out."

Each put their sunglasses on and strolled at a leisurely pace toward the park at the center of town.

Aprell opened her eyes, blinked and gazed at the scenery rushing past. Shifting in her seat, she caught Evan glancing at her. He smiled and quickly looked away.

"How was your nap?" Evan asked.

"Good," Aprell answered, stretching as best she could given her cramped space. "Why were you watching me?"

"Habit." Evan glanced at her again. "Doctor mode doesn't shut down. It's integral to who I am. Like your magic is."

"Oh, you think so?" Aprell slipped her shoes off, wriggling her toes.

"Yes, I do. How do you explain it?"

She thought about her fast, quick response she would have rattled off. Telling Evan magic could be turned on or off wouldn't make sense. It hadn't to her grandmother either. Learning to control her magical traits had taken time and a lot of work. Effort that had her sweating and swearing in Latin and the few choice words her Brazilian college roommate had taught her. Evan had asked. She needed to explain as best she could.

"You don't know this. I struggled to find out what my magic is. Being a late bloomer isn't easy."

"Is that why you got ostracized and cut out from the popular groups?"

"A part of it."

"Damn, I didn't know."

Aprell snickered. "Not many did or do. Not even my grandmother."

Evan pulled up to the light and stopped. He glanced at her, shook his head and laid his hand on her arm. "Wow. Thanks for sharing. Fitting in is hard when you're different."

"Oh yeah. I get that part. I remember the pranks they thought were funny and weren't." Aprell pulled her knees up to her and turned toward Evan more. "Please explain again how I'm supposed to help with grandmother."

Evan clasped the steering wheel and eased into traffic until he could easily make the right turn onto the four-lane highway leading them out into the rural farmland that brought them closer to Sylvan Valley. "I let you sleep longer than forty-five minutes."

Aprell's mouth dropped open. He couldn't miss that glare even if he had a pair of blinders like a horse drawing a buggy wore. Her face grew redder with every huffing breath she took. He knew that look. The exasperated, pissed and ready-to-explode one that, if he didn't say something soon, might contain angry words that weren't necessary. Well, not necessary as far as he was concerned. "*I needed time to think on that.* I'm not sure how much help you're going to be or if you're being here is going to be all that's needed."

"You need to explain that gibberish."

Evan pressed his lips tighter together. Aprell hadn't lost her favorite word. The one that defined most of their junior and senior high years when their fellow classmates were busy perfecting their magic basics and yammering in Latin or other dialects based upon the spell type they were studying. "I know. I'm still not sure, except that our grandmothers listen to us. Focus on what we say to a point."

"That's true. But you know they're stubborn. They can out-mule us hands down."

Evan laughed. "*Oh, can they.* I want the best for Tia Maxi. Maybe it's time she stops living alone. Gets a roommate."

"At her age, she hasn't given up looking." Aprell turned back in her seat facing forward.

"Looking for what?" Evan shot a sideways glance at Aprell. She kept looking straight ahead. He opened his mouth ready to scramble to cover his dumb remark. Abada had told him more than once to not snoop in her bathroom medicine chest. Had he listened? No, he hadn't. She had condoms, lube and a vibrating cock ring in there. He swallowed hard and tried to speak. "Yo-you don't need to answer that."

"Oh, but I do. You asked, and we agreed on honesty between you and me." Aprell shot him a shit-eating grin that rivaled any illustrations of the

Cheshire cat he'd seen in the kids' books in his waiting room. Damn, he'd stepped in it deep when he agreed honesty between them was fundamental to their discussion. Fuck, he hadn't known it would end up here. Discussing Abada and Tia Maxi's sex lives. Talk about TMI!

"Really, you don't need to answer that." He inhaled sharply, gulping air as best he could. Gripping the steering wheel tighter until his hands hurt, he kept looking ahead, hoping Aprell wasn't looking at him grinning more.

Aprell pressed her teeth against her tongue, ready to tease Evan more. She'd caught the way he clasped the steering wheel. His hands were almost paper-white. Given his paleness, that told her a lot. He wasn't comfortable with the topic at hand. Most medical personnel she talked with didn't have a problem discussing sex. Most encouraged their older patients or clients to seek out companionship and talk about STDs and safe sex practices. Evan hadn't been a prude during their teen years. In fact, he brought up the topic of sex more than once. A couple of times to pluck her nerve or see if he could embarrass her. Of course, the time she'd caught her grandparents making out like two hot horny youths, she'd stammered and blushed, trying to tell him about it. She sucked in air, almost biting her tongue. That was it. Talking about her grandmother's love life also put his abada's on report too. She pressed her lips together tightly. Mirth threatened to spill out. Talk about ironical. He'd teased and plucked her about almost the same thing in high school. Oh, wow what a time for karma to declare payback time.

"Evan, I'm sorry." Aprell reached out toward Evan, watching the road as well. Distracting him as he drove wasn't part of her solution. Admitting she'd oopsed was all she wanted to do. They pulled up to a stop sign. She leaned over, laid her hand on Evan's arm, and continued speaking. "I ribbed you without realizing we brought Tia Donya into this. Didn't mean to."

Evan looked at her, nodded, and shrugged. "I'm not a prude. Being a doctor, you can't be. Well, you gotta be open to talking about lots of things. Abada and Tia Maxi's love life wasn't one I had planned on."

Aprell snickered. "Truth is, neither had I. I thought you knew Grandmother and Mr. Yost are sorta courting to quote her."

"No, I didn't know Tia Maxi has a boyfriend. Abada tried to tell me about her boyfriend and I said TMI and walked away."

Aprell shook her head. "Why does that bother you?"

"Well, it's getting used to the idea your parents have sex. Then you think, oh shit, my grandparents had sex. Maybe still do. It boggles the mind when it gets closer up and personal." Evan glanced at her, patted her hand and took it off his arm. "Now that we're past the oh man, that is a delicate topic, what is going on with Tia Maxi finding a roommate?"

Aprell settled back in her seat. "She's ready to date to quote her. Mr. Yost has shown an interest in her. He's a few years younger. I've heard a lot about him and another gentleman that spend time playing poker with them at the Relief Society Socials as well as dancing."

"Is this the same Mr. Yost who let her ride a skateboard down the street?"

"I don't know. If he did, I've got a few things to say to him. Grandmother isn't that young."

Evan looked at her, laughed and looked away. "I'm sure you'll find out soon enough. We're about forty-five minutes away."

"I hear Tia Donya has a few gentlemen interested in her, too."

"I don't need to hear about this," Evan blurted out almost running a red light.

"Oh, why not Evan?" Aprell looked at him, stuck out her tongue and blew a raspberry at him. "PFFFFT if you've become that prudish. It's not getting naked and asking for a blow-by-blow tell-all confession."

"No, it's not. Abada's love life is her own business. Not mine." Evan faced her, pointing a finger at her just like he used to do when she'd struck one of his core ethics. Except when it came to sex, he didn't want to learn about magics' facts of life. Problem was he never got that they did it the same way mortals did. Genetics, conception and all the associated medical basics remained the same. Differences came in on the extra pairs of chromosomes that split and spliced on their own. Some unique magic traits bonded and came about. Like Henry Smith who couldn't spell cast unless he levitated or shapeshifted. His fire mage lineage paid off when he went into conservation and firefighting.

"Evan," Aprell began, flexing her hands lest she clench them tight and break a nail. Evan would know how frustrated she was. "Knowing about Mr. Yost and his interest is *not* an issue. *We* both know our grandmothers don't want us knowing about the intimate details."

Evan kept silent. He'd teased his grandmother about his love life and let loose with a few innuendos. So what made it wrong for her to do the same?

Why was one different from the other? Thinking about Abada in a mortal aspect didn't fit his experience? Was he that narrow-minded that he couldn't see her as anything other than a magical being? Deities above, when had that happened?

He cleared his throat as he turned onto Main Street. "Five more miles to go until we're there. It's slow going with these rural roads. I've got a confession to make."

"*Huh? You do?*" Aprell turned so she faced him.

He pulled into a parking place close to the small shopping district at the edge of the strip mall. "Yes. It's between us. If Abada finds out, she'll be hurt. Tia Maxi and Tia Tabby, too."

Aprell laid a hand on his arm. "What about me?"

"I can't say. You'll tell me after I've said it." Evan put the car into park. "When I'm done, I'd like to walk a bit and center. How about an ice cream?"

Aprell nodded, gripping his arm tighter. "Sure."

He unfastened his seat belt and faced Aprell. "I don't know how or why I've become bigoted. Narrow-minded."

Aprell pulled away, covered her mouth with her hand, shaking her head.

"You find this funny?" Evan narrowed his eyes, glaring at her.

"No. It's not funny like a joke. It's ironical though."

"How so?" Evan folded his arms almost hugging himself tightly.

Aprell took two breaths, held the last and gathered her thoughts. Watching someone confront their prejudices often didn't turn out well. She'd seen that happen more than once when the Witch Council elders called several of their graduating class out on incidents that crossed lines into maliciousness. Growth happened for some. Others. . .well, they apologized and ostracized themselves because they thought they were superior. Evan couldn't help some of what he felt based on how he'd been treated.

"You're realizing things that others take for granted and vice versa. You can't beat yourself up for your experience. You can change, grow into a new view and way of being."

Evan nodded. "God, I feel like one of those bobbleheads we collected on our senior trip to Chicago."

Aprell tittered. "Are you ready to accept you belong and are part of Sylvan Valley's mixed community or are you still standing on the outside longing to belong?"

"What about when someone magics me?" Evan opened his door and got out.

That was a good question. Some spells had fallout that many didn't realize. Even knowing this, magic wasn't precise like some things. Aprell wondered if Evan realized practicing medicine and magic shared many nuances. Bumped up against each other in those gray areas.

"There's no pat answer. You know the oaths and loyalty we all swore as we came into our abilities and graduated. Isn't that like your medical oath and license to practice medicine?" She exited the car and stood on the sidewalk.

Evan stepped up beside her. He held out his hand. "True. I'm not jeopardizing my license and what I love to do."

Aprell took hold of Evan's hand. Heat crossed her palm, wrapping its tendrils around her wrist. She inhaled, squeezed Evan's hand and pressed her palm against his. "There are many magics who feel the same way. Even supernaturals. We all want tranquility, to live our lives amongst family and friends who care about us, and be part of a community that provides and protects our well being."

"I know many who honor that. Abada having a boyfriend is going to take getting used to. That is one conversation I'm going to have to work up to having with her."

"If she hasn't told you yet, I'm sure she's not ready to blurt it out either." Aprell let go of Evan's hand, pulled open the door to the ice cream shop, and entered. She stopped the door from closing, faced Evan and added. "Just like we don't need to tell about the heat and reactions we've had on the ride home."

Evan blinked, frowned and shrugged. He walked past her into the shop. Pushing him for a verbal response wasn't going to happen. She'd gotten one nonetheless. He'd felt something, too. What she didn't know. For now, they'd shared a companionable space of time together, even discussed things like they had growing up. Where things went from here, neither of them knew. Maybe this time, they'd figure it out on their own without family, friends, or magic interfering.

Twenty minutes passed as they sat outside the shop, eating their sundaes. Chocolate sauce and fudge ripple ice cream for her. Strawberries, hot fudge sauce, and Neapolitan ice cream made up Evan's. Another ten passed as they walked back to the car and got underway again. Watching the colors change and twilight fall as they drove along the rural roads leading home reminded her of one thing. Coming home was magical in itself.

CHAPTER SEVEN

Aprell pressed her lips together as Evan turned onto Main Street. Words failed her. Images rushed over her kindling memories. Forgotten incidents that flashed and fleeted. She swallowed, wet her lips and tried putting her thoughts into words. "The park is still here. The center of the circle. There's city hall. The library and—whoa! That's new." She pointed at the four-story building across from where they stopped.

"Sylvan Valley has grown. That's the hospital. Two streets over is my office and two new medical buildings. Last year the state redistricted the county lines. Welcome to the county seat." Evan continued down Main Street a bit further. "Remember Birchette Elementary?"

"I sure do." Aprell pointed at the building ahead of them on the left. "They added to the school."

"Yup. Read the sign." Evan slowed the car as they passed.

"Sylvan Valley High School?" Aprell looked at Evan. "When?"

"Four years ago. Redistricting became the watchdog word at state, county and local levels. As more supernaturals revealed their existence, towns like ours grew."

"I heard something about dividing the town in two. Please tell me prejudice hasn't gotten more ugly around here." Aprell shook her head. "Goddess, I hope not."

"Oh, there's still a few on both sides who think separate but equal should be the norm. It's not." Evan picked up speed as they crossed the city line and a large blue and white state sign.

"The sign said leaving Sylvan Valley city limits. That isn't right. The city limits are middle of the street out past Cumberpatch Hill Roundabout." Aprell's mouth hung open.

"Not since redistricting and the state line moved again." Evan slowed down as they approached a stop sign. He pointed to the street signs on the corner. "Main and Prairie. Still the same names. Passes through many of the same neighborhoods and areas we grew up with."

"State line moved?" Aprell asked, not sure how local politics ever did more than confuse and tinker with things like county lines and if people lived in or out of the city. Taxes must have gone up.

"Surveyors found that historical documents and records didn't match so they hemmed and debated for six months until they compromised. Stutter's Creek is the new boundary border."

"What that puts our neighborhood in..."

Evan laughed. "Nothing like the state line running down middle of your living room?"

"They didn't? Did they?"

"No. Divided the city into Sylvan Valley and New Sylvan Valley a mile over the state border. We're in the unincorporated area dubbed Sylvan Valley Township."

"Politicians. Always messing with something." Aprell let go a pent-up sigh and slumped in her seat. "I guess nothing stays the same."

Evan covered her hand with his. "My first few years back from med school reeled me. Change was at the top of everyone's priority list. Then it settled down again. Even with the divisions, unity remains strong with folks turning out for elections, city council meetings and the yearly celebration in the park."

Aprell leaned over put her other hand on Evan's and squeezed, pressing his hand against both of hers. "I'm silly to expect change hadn't happened. If I wanted it all to remain the same, I should've stuck around."

"It would have come even with that. Our families are some of the first that championed change and embracing new things. I hope they can embrace change and find new ways to stay vital and vibrant."

"Speaking of change, do we let on we've talked?" Aprell let go of Evan's hand.

Evan took hold of the steering wheel and eased the car into the traffic flow leading away from the city. "I don't think we need to. They're going to assume whether we tell them or not."

"Okay. So we just nod like we've always done and let them go on?"

"No. We can't change their minds if they think we're going to go along with stuff. We hear them out. I doubt they're going to have much to say. Remember, Tia Maxi is our main focus."

Aprell nodded. "I'll deal with my grandmother. You deal with yours and in between we'll deal with the three of them as needed."

Evan chortled. "More like keeping an eye on them at all times. We don't need magiced by them or anyone else again."

"I know you think they used and do use magic without thinking sometimes. I don't believe that to be true." Aprell held up her hand as he opened his mouth to reply. "I'm not arguing with you. Your experience is your own. Let's make sure we've got the facts before we say anything is all I'm saying."

"Agreed," Evan responded. Did Aprell understand he'd overheard more than one discussion about them being so right for each other growing up? He wasn't getting matched or magiced again. He'd make his mate choice on his own, the mortal way—attraction, chemistry and hormones. Though why he missed the pings, zings and warmth Aprell jolted him with today when they were growing up, he didn't know.

Quiet mixed with the sense of contentment welling up within him. He kept glancing at Aprell as he drove. Until she caught him, winked, and smiled. He hadn't expected this feeling. The attraction. The ease with their conversation. And his desire to explore the undercurrent flowing off them when they touched. Was this there before? A natural chemistry instead of magic lingering in the background, whether he imagined it or it was really there. He inhaled, ready to ask when Aprell spoke.

"Thank you for hearing me out. I know it's hard to feel understood when you feel you don't fit in." Aprell wanted to reassure Evan everything would work out. Turn out for the best with her grandmother accepting her age step and the changes she needed to make. Aprell knew her grandmother couldn't. Nothing prepared a magical person for the change when it happened. It wasn't aging or physical changes that stressed them. The loss of magic rattled a magical more than anything else. It was their core sense of being, what set them apart that ignited their growth and maturity. It also signaled their change, the slowdown that left them less talented than before. Losing part of themselves didn't come with a sense of balance or approval. It wasn't easy to explain. Could she put it into words Evan could relate to? She wasn't sure. This was going to take some thought.

"You're welcome. We're almost there. I'm going to come in with you. Abada is probably there," Evan said.

Aprell took a deep breath, flexed her fingers and nodded. She'd bet he was avoiding something. She didn't know what, nor was she going to ask. She'd already picked up on some of his nervousness the closer they got to Appleby Drive and her grandmother's house.

Maxi paced the area between the couch and the kitchen doorway for a third time. She looked at the grandfather clock as she walked up to the front door, opened it and looked out. She closed the door, sighed and walked back to the couch. As she sat down, she pointed at Donya. *"Are you sure we can trust Evan with Aprell?"*

Donya looked up from her knitting. She laid her needlework in her lap. "You think the two of them eloped? Are banging in some roadside hotel?"

Tabby's snort and chortle drew squinted-eyed stares from both of them. "Sorry," she said and went back to leafing through the magazine she'd been looking at.

"You think that's funny?" Maxi pointed at Donya again. "The two of them fought like cats and dogs the last time they were together."

Donya shook her head and faced her. "That was what? Ten? Twelve years ago? I find it hard to believe that either of them is still experiencing teenage hormonal angst."

Maxi lowered her hand. "I'm projecting again, aren't I?"

Tabby laid her magazine on the coffee table. "You're worried. At odds over things. Nothing is the same, and yet in some ways it is."

"I agree. Evan and Aprell are going to have their spats and outbursts. We did at their ages, too. Errol and I did throughout our marriage. He picked a fight with me a week before he passed. Said he wanted his spitfire alive and not mourning." Donya picked up her knitting and resumed counting stitches.

Maxi bunched part of her skirt in her good hand. Her granddaughter was going to walk through the front door any moment, and the world as she knew it would change forever. How did anyone make peace with that? This wasn't a planned visit. An overly joyous event both of them looked forward to. What the change would be, Maxi didn't know. Magic often worked the same way with known spells and incantations. Things changed when someone tried a new or different way of doing magic. Their point of view changed, and how they went about things changed, too. Maybe that was what scared her the most. She'd have to become someone she didn't know. Someone so uniquely different that it frightened her. How did a two-hundred-year-old witch admit she was scared?

Maxi glanced at Donya, then Tabby. They'd learned in their teens what losing magic looked like when their great-grandparents started losing theirs. She hadn't. Her family hid that truth from her until her grandfather called a family meeting to announce he'd divorced Grandma because she couldn't twitch. Couldn't cast a spell worth manure. Most of her spells had turned into fertilizer. That kept the bills paid. Her family had tried to hide their purist views. Fitting in mattered. Maxi let go of her skirt. Smoothed her hand over it and tried to smile. Her trust outweighed her fear. Her trust that Aprell, Donya, and Tabby wouldn't abandon her. She knew Evan wouldn't. He'd taken care of her after she fell. He showed his support with love and actions just like Aprell, Donya and Tabby had and would. Maxi knew her fear came from not knowing, and this was one area not any of them could predict the outcome.

"I suppose I should own my fears, quirks and worries." Maxi smoothed her other hand down and across her skirt. "I can't change what's happening. Might as well just accept it."

"Being a bit maudlin, Maxi?" Tabby asked. "I understand your regret, your worry, and your uncertainty. Maybe the chillax, as my niece says to all this, is you go with the flow and err on the side of caution?"

Maxi opened her mouth to reply as a hard knock sounded on the front door.

Donya put her knitting in an open bag sitting near her feet. "If that's Evan, why is he knocking?"

"Because he gave me back my key," Maxi said, trying to stand up.

"He did?" Donya stood, holding her hand out to her.

Maxi gripped it and shakily rose. "He felt it better that I give Aprell my extra key than him. He said no need for unnecessary explanations." Maxi stood straighter, smoothed her hands down her skirt and slowly moved around the coffee table.

Tabby patted her arm as she moved passed her, adding her thoughts on Evan returning the key. "No telling how those two have interacted on the ride from the airport. Smoke could precede them."

Donya walked past Tabby and Maxi, shaking her head. "I think Evan has much better manners than you give him credit for. He wouldn't pick a fight with Aprell."

Maxi laughed. "I agree. Aprell has manners, too. We *do know* how heated their discussion can get. I don't think we have to worry about sparks or smoke this time."

A harder knock rattled the door. "If we don't open the door, sparks and smoke might start," Donya added as she moved up next to Maxi. "Don't need either of them worrying."

Maxi undid the bolt lock and grasped the door with her good hand. As she opened it, setting sunlight streamed in, blocking her vision. She blinked, squinted, and smiled.

Aprell startled as the loud click followed by a squeak as the door of the house she'd moved away from opened. As the door opened wider, her grandmother came into view. She looked the same in many ways, Curly hair, flowered skirt and single-colored top matching one of the skirt's predominant colors—Aprell swallowed hard as her grandmother stepped onto the porch. Gone was the strawberry blonde hair that as a child, she thought magically glowed every time her grandmother smiled. Salt and pepper-colored curls lay in ringlets on her grandmother's head. Her smile still beamed like a hundred-watt light bulb just like it had every time her grandmother greeted her. The other thing that stood out was the stark white cast on her left arm. Aprell blinked, pressing her lips together tighter. She reached back until she brushed Evan's hand. He entwined his fingers with hers and lightly pressed his palm against hers. Sparks sizzled as warmth circled around her wrist and faded. Magic had signaled something. What she didn't have time to decipher. Her grandmother was talking to her.

"Aprell! You made it." Maxi moved toward her, spreading her arms wide. There was no missing her grimace as she tried to raise her left arm higher.

Aprell released Evan's hand and stepped into her grandmother's embrace. "Yes. Glad to be here and not in the air."

Aprell wrapped her arms around her grandmother loosely. Their usual tight hugs that lasted several moments didn't seem appropriate. Only because she didn't want to hurt her grandmother.

Maxi lowered her right arm and tried to step back, reaching for her left. "Guess I'm going to need a bit of help with this."

"Let me help," Evan offered, reaching between Tia Maxi and Aprell.

"Thank you, Evan." Maxi turned so she faced Aprell.

Aprell put on her best fake smile. She knew her grandmother could read it as well as if she had sarcastically said something.

"Aprell. Evan," Tia Donya stepped onto the porch. Aprell glanced away, inhaled quickly and exhaled, trying to push her doubts and fears away from her. Not knowing and yet not voicing her thoughts were two different things.

"Slowly lower your arm, Tia Maxi, until it's even with my hand." Evan held his hand out, palm up.

Aprell flexed her hands every time her grandmother winched. Seconds slowed as if time flowed through gelatin. Slow, sticky and very intense.

Maxi grimaced again as she laid her arm on Evan's hand.

'Good. Now clasp your other hand with mine." Evan moved closer to her grandmother. Aprell pressed her lips tighter together, pushing her need to jump in and help out of her thoughts. Evan knew what he was doing. This was his realm. His area of expertise, physical medicine that needed mortal oversight. Magic healed in many ways, as did tried and true heart and knowledge medicine.

Tia Maxi clasped his hand tightly. Evan steadied himself. "Take your time and move toward me."

Tia Maxi moved closer until there were only a few inches between them. "Good," Evan said, letting go of Tia Maxi's hand. "Take hold of your cast and slowly lower your arm. I'm here to lean on or catch you."

Her grandmother grasped her cast and slowly lowered her arm. Aprell intently watched Evan and her grandmother. His focus was on his patient and someone he cared about. Magic didn't put him off. His patient needed him. Maybe he had changed. Aprell took a step forward as her grandmother wobbled. Evan got to her first, slipping his arm around her waist. Aprell glanced at Tia Donya, who nodded. This was a side of Evan Aprell hadn't seen before. Just as her hometown had changed, grown and transformed into a new city that readily embraced who its citizens were, maybe she and Evan had done the same. The sparks of attraction were definitely hotter and stronger than the last time they were together.

"Easy, Tia Maxi." Evan stopped when he was toe-to-toe with her. "Let me know what you need me to do."

"I'm not sure. This is harder than I thought." Maxi took a deep breath. Evan noted how tired she looked. Or was she giving up? None of his grandmother's posse gave up. They kept going. Lending each other energy and the push they needed to succeed. They were closer than blood siblings. They were magical siblings without the blood link that heightened the link even more. Together, their magic was stronger.

"Getting used to the cast takes time." Evan glanced at Aprell. She nodded. Maybe their talk in the car helped dispel their preconceptions, opening more straightforward communication between them.

"It sure does." Maxi clutched Aprell's arm. "I think I better sit down."

Aprell glanced at Evan. His gaze met hers. He shook his head and shrugged. What had her grandmother spooked?

CHAPTER EIGHT

Donya loaded the last of the dinner dishes into the dishwasher. Chef Mario had outdone himself with the welcome home dinner he prepared and delivered. Donya faced Tabby. "Something has Maxi spooked."

"She's never subdued." Tabby dried her hands on the towel hanging on the oven door handle. "She didn't say much during dinner. Barely ate."

"And in bed before eleven." Donya sat in one of the kitchen table chairs.

"Do you think we should stay or go home like she kept telling us to?" Tabby sat across from her.

"She wasn't in any pain." Donya laid her hands on the table. "Evan said it might be a reality drop. Maxi's feeling sorry for herself. Aprell is here."

"She can't fool herself?" Tabby glanced at her watch.

"Could be part of it." Donya sighed and leaned back in her chair. "Accepting she needs help, needs time to heal, and that she's aged all at once isn't a small pill to swallow."

"Not for any of us to swallow." Tabby yawned. "Probably best we stay here tonight."

Donya nodded. "I found a container of hot chocolate mix as I was making dinner. That and a few cookies are a great bedtime snack. I'll heat the water. You get Aprell and Evan."

Tabby rose. "Change is happening. Yet there's a hint of nostalgia about."

"Aprell and Evan together again. Not the same people, for sure. We're all older and more experienced." Donya filled the tea kettle and set it on the stove. She turned the burner under the kettle on. "I suspect we're all in for more changes."

Tabby put her hand on the kitchen door, ready to push it open. She lowered her hand and turned back to Donya. "Maybe the future gateway, the One and Deities are opening is one that we've got to step through. I've got a feeling it's going to take all of us on a journey of discovery."

Donya set four mugs on the table along with the hot chocolate mix container, spoons and the box of cookies. "I agree. We're probably two steps through the gateway already."

Aprell exited the guest room next to her grandmother's bedroom. The house hadn't changed much. Redecorating had happened. New colors. A few new pieces of furniture. Different placement of pictures and furniture arrangement. Homecoming wasn't about going back in time. Nothing stayed the same. She knew that. Accepted it. Yet, part of her longed for the comfort of the past in some ways. She'd left here a young woman ready to take on the world. She'd returned older, wiser, and possibly surer of who she was and what she wanted out of life. Talking with Evan today had ignited a yearning to see if they could reconnect. Reconnect as friends? Extended family members? Or—*more*, her conscience whispered. Aprell shook her head and continued into the living room.

Evan sat on the couch reading the newspaper. One thing he swore in high school he'd never do. Evening newscast, via TV or radio, was enough for him. Their senior year, they'd learned how reading could relax them. Different topics cleared their mind, took them places that their classroom learning didn't.

Aprell perched on the arm of the couch opposite Evan. "Anything interesting?"

Evan lowered the paper. "Somedays, it's more of the same. Dismal and gloomy. I refuse to do more than read the front page headlines and go straight for the comics and crossword puzzle."

"We get clobbered daily with our jobs. Health care, mental and physical, is demanding." Aprell took the paper from Evan and stuffed it in the trash can close to the fireplace. "Make great kindling."

Evan chuckled. "Yeah, sure does. I feel for Tia Maxi. She's gobsmacked with so much in the last few days."

The kitchen door swung open. Tabby entered the living room. "Come on for a bedtime snack. Cookies and hot chocolate."

Evan rose, dusted his hands on his jeans, and started toward the kitchen. He paused, waiting for Aprell to catch up with him. "I'm next door if you need me."

"Grandmother is your landlord." Aprell grinned and added, "Thank you for that."

"You bet." Evan held the kitchen door open. "Put my cell phone number in your phone. Call if you need me."

Donya filled the mugs and set the tea kettle back on the stove. She sat in the chair closest to her. She pointed to the other chairs. "Aprell, Evan and Tabby, please sit. Help yourself to hot chocolate and cinnamon crisp cookies."

Tabby put napkins on the table and sat across from Donya. "Donya and I are staying tonight. We're in the room at the end of the hall."

"I appreciate everything you've done for Grandmother. I'm sure there's plenty I need to know. Tia Donya and Tia Tabby with you here, I can sleep easier tonight." Aprell sat close to Evan. She laid her cell phone on the table. Evan picked it up and added his phone number to her contacts. Any other time, she'd fuss. There was a difference tonight. It was all of them taking care of each other. Supporting family and friends.

Evan yawned and stretched. He broke a cookie in half. "I'm heading home in a few. Tia Maxi should sleep the night through. She took pain meds before she got into bed."

Aprell handed Evan a packet of hot chocolate mix. " Evan, Tia Donya and Tia Tabby, thank you for taking care of grandmother."

Donya emptied her packet into her mug and stirred. "Family takes care of each other."

"What Donya said." Tabby sipped her hot chocolate and placed a cookie on a napkin. "Evan helped the most."

Evan slid Aprell's phone across the table to her. "I did what any physician would do. Take care of those that need us."

"Evan," Aprell began, pulling her phone to her. "You stepped up. Didn't wait for a magical physician to show up or the ambulance."

"Times have changed. Medical practitioners, whether magical or mortal, practice medicine pretty much the same. Take care of your patients' immediate needs." Evan popped part of his cookie into his mouth and chewed.

Aprell nodded. "You're correct. I forget sometimes that magics and mortals accept each other for who they are. Not what they are."

Donya dunked her cookie in her hot chocolate. "I think what we need to focus on is taking care of each other. Making sure Maxi gets the care, support and information she needs to decide what's next."

"Agreed." Tabby sipped her hot chocolate and set her mug down. "I sent an email to a friend at the Relief Society."

Evan pulled his mug to him, added a hot chocolate packet and stirred. "Tia Maxi's exam shows she needs time to heal physically. She's not in immediate need of supervised or twenty-four-seven care. I don't think she needs to move to the Relief Society."

"I checked on services available." Tabby ate the rest of her cookie, wiped her fingers and laid her napkin on the table. "Home health care is something many of the society members want."

Donya nodded. "Mrs. Tuttle mentioned this at the last thrift store board meeting. She's on the Relief Society board, too."

Evan drank part of his hot chocolate. "Okay, here is what I'm suggesting. Over the next couple of weeks, let's see what's available for Tia Maxi."

Aprell pushed her empty mug to the middle of the table. "Sounds like we're agreed on a fact-finding mission. See what happens over the next few weeks and assess what we find out."

Evan stood, stretched and yawned. "Sounds like a plan. I've got to run. I've got a consult in Cauldron Falls midmorning. Need some beauty sleep before then."

Donya rose and hugged Evan. "Be safe Evan. Te querio mucho."

"Love you, too, Abada." Evan hugged Abada and faced Aprell. "Thanks for an interesting conversation this afternoon. Call me if you or Tia Maxi need anything."

"I'll walk you to the door." Aprell followed Evan out of the kitchen.

Donya glanced at Tabby. Tabby shrugged.

"There's something going on between them." Donya put the mugs and spoons in the sink.

Tabby put the cookies and hot chocolate mix away. She wiped down the table. "That's between them. Last time we got involved, sparks flew, magic backfired, and we got told off."

"Whatever it is, I'm sure they can handle it." Donya pushed the chairs back to the table. "I hope."

Aprell paused as she and Evan reached the front door. "I probably should have asked this earlier. Is there anything you haven't told the others I need to know?"

Evan opened the front door. "Let's talk out on the porch."

Aprell followed Evan onto the porch, closing the door behind them. She faced Evan. He perched on the porch railing. "Nothing that I haven't told them in simpler terms. Tia Maxi needs to slow down. She needs companionship. Abada and Tia Tabby as well. They need each other and more."

"Are you saying they need chaperoning?" Aprell dropped onto the wicker bench across from Evan.

"Nothing like that." Evan stood, walked over and sat next to her. "They can't be together twenty-four seven. I asked Abada about that. She told me they tried that *one time*. Said I didn't need to know more than tried."

Aprell smiled. "I know what you're talking about. They rented a two-bedroom furnished apartment with a sofa sleeper. That lasted six months before they decided living together wasn't a good idea."

"Sleeper sofa?" Evan shook his head. "If it was anything like the apartment I shared during medical school, no wonder they said not *ever* again."

"Now I've got to ask. What happened?" Aprell leaned closer to Evan.

"Twelve hours on. Twelve hours off. This is not unusual during residency and internship." Evan sighed. "Like it is after med school sometimes. Anywho, I got to the apartment, shucked my clothes and dropped into bed."

"No big deal." Aprell started to stand.

Evan put his hand on her arm. "There's more. Two hours later, I'm jolted awake by cold feet and hands touching me."

Aprell cocked her head, arching an eyebrow, gawking him like he was bullshitting her.

"My roommate's girlfriend was in the wrong bed. She'd driven all night and didn't know Ted and I had changed rooms. Try jumping out of bed buck naked and not scare the crap out of both of you. One of Ted's friends was passed out on the couch. Ted stumbled out of his room, holding a pillow in front of him."

Aprell snickered, looked down and back up.

Evan nodded. "Ted and I took the bedroom doors off to paint them. We'd never got them hung back up. That night was one that made the rounds of the hospital. Ted and I got a stern lecture from the head of the ER. Ted's friend laughed so hard he fell off the couch and bruised himself in areas we vowed not to discuss."

Aprell wiped her eyes. "Oh my. Some would say you made it up."

Evan held his hand up, palm toward the sky. "I swear by the Goddess, it's true. Our lease was up three months later. We definitely decided renewing wasn't in our mutual best interests."

"I haven't laughed that hard in a while. Thank you." Aprell smiled and knuckled a tear off her cheek. "One of life's absurdities. I'll share one."

"Sure." Evan scooted closer to Aprell.

"Nancy, my business partner, left in a rush to get to the bank before closing and get to a family wedding. She didn't tell me she'd turned on the alarm system." Aprell smirked and shook her head. "I open the shop's front door to let the alarm service technician in to change batteries in two of the sensors. Every alarm goes off. Took us ten minutes to get them turned off and convince police dispatch everything was okay."

"Got a lecture from the police chief?"

"And our insurance agent. We now have keychain fobs to arm and disarm the alarm system."

Evan stood. "Life's challenges. We get through them and learn."

Aprell rose. "Sure do. I wish you deep sleep and dream well Evan."

Evan moved closer to Aprell. He put his arm around her shoulders, hugging her tightly. "There's something I've been wanting to do since we stopped at the rest stop."

"What?"

Evan cupped Aprell's face with both hands, leaned in and pressed his lips to hers. He pulled back, lowered his hands, and kissed Aprell again. "Only our magic this time."

Aprell touched her lips. She moved closer to Evan. "Our magic. I'm returning your kiss."

Aprell looped her arms around Evan's neck, tilted her head, and puckered her lips. Evan brushed his lips across hers. He placed his hands on her waist, moving until the space between them was nill. Only their clothing separated their flesh. Evan leaned in, pressing his lips against hers again. Aprell parted her lips, tracing the seam of Evan's lips with the tip of her tongue. Evan drew her tighter to him. He pulled his head back a bit.

"Are you sure?" Evan slowly inhaled and exhaled. His chest pressing against her. "We've been here before."

Aprell nodded. "Very sure."

Evan pressed closer, tighter to Aprell. Every breath each of them took pressed them against each other. Heat swirled around them, enveloping them in its elusive pull where only the two of them existed. Evan inhaled deeply, seeing wasps of color flash into being and explode like fireworks across the night sky. His eyes closed as his lips met Aprell's. Her lips parted. Their tongues met. Evan sipped and tasted chocolate and cinnamon. Aprell's essence filled his nostrils. Abada said every person exuded their personal pheromones that attracted and marked the person they were interested in and attracted to. Evan inhaled deeper. Images of the first bouquet he'd given Aprell flashed through his mind. White and yellow daisies wildflowers he picked as they walked along the creek flowing in the woods behind the school. A hint of cinnamon lingered. Maybe it was his own tastebuds picking up bits and pieces of the lingering chocolate and cookies in his mouth. It didn't matter. No magic other than their own brought them to this point. This place and moment. He savored one last lingering sip and broke off the kiss.

"Wow," Aprell whispered. "We still got it?"

Evan smiled and brushed his lips over Aprell's again. "Is it still? Or we've grown and changed?"

Aprell opened her mouth to answer. Evan pressed his fingers against Aprell's lips. "Think on it. Sleep on it. We'll talk more. I'm heading home and to bed."

Aprell nodded, kissed his fingers, and walked into the house. Evan flexed his hands, trotting down the front steps and across the yard to his apartment building. He doubted his sleep would be dreamless.

CHAPTER NINE

A week without a word from Evan. Forty-eight hours since his brief text. *Stuck in Cauldron Falls.* Not that it was a bad thing. The physician and patient he was helping needed him. Aprell slumped lower against the wicker bench on the porch. Waiting and watching she kept saying she wasn't doing. Here she was, glancing toward Evan's apartment building every time a car slowed or turned into the building's parking lot. Her heart did a *pitter-patter* dance, hoping the person getting out of the car was him. She knew from talking with Tia Donya, Evan focused on his patients and what they needed. Tia Tabby and her grandmother were walking around the block like the orthopedist, Dr. Kenneth Maxwell, had prescribed. Keeping active was intergral to her grandmother staying limber and positive.

Lunch and reminiscing with Kenneth had taken away part of the loneliness Aprell felt. Kenneth explained what he saw happening with her grandmother. She'd reached a point where being alone wasn't good for her. Friends, activities and having someone to date were essential to a magic's mental and physical well-being. Aprell sighed. Kenneth had patted her hand and kissed her cheek after he suggested keeping her grandmother company on her walks might be good for both of them. Kenneth reminded her physicans, like he and Evan, were known for their tunnel vision when it came to their patients and their practice.

Aprell entered the house. Sitting and watching the apartment building wasn't going to make Evan appear. She had business emails to answer, calls to make and check in with Nancy. Running a business from afar wasn't easy. It didn't take a lot of effort. The effort came from time zone differences and connecting with her clients via videoconferencing. Upgrading her grandmother's internet account was the easy part. Paying a year in advance made sense even though Aprell didn't know if she'd be here in a year.

Aprell filled the tea kettle, set it on the stove and turned the burner under it on. Tea hot and sweet and the leftover grilled ham and cheese sandwich from last night's dinner would help her focus. She put the sandwich to warm in the microwave and set a mug on the counter. Aprell calculated the time between

Sylvan Valley and Honolulu. She had approximately twenty minutes until her next client meeting.

A hard knock rattled the back door, rousing Aprell from her thoughts. She glanced out the kitchen window. An older man stood on the back porch holding a basket of apples and peaches under one arm and a small bouquet of pink and yellow tulips in his hand. Neither Tia Donya nor Tia Tabby had mentioned grandmother had a gentleman admirer going to drop by. Aprell reached for the door as another knock sounded. Sounds from the living room flowed into the kitchen. Tia Tabby and Grandmother Maxi were back.

"Grandmother Maxi, there's a gentleman at the back door," Aprell called out.

Tabby ran to the door and looked out and back as Maxi entered the kitchen. "It's Mr. Yost."

Maxi hobbled to the door, smiling; she unlocked the door and opened it. "Daniel Yost. What are you doing here?"

"Darlin' checking on ye." Daniel held out the bouquet of flowers. "Matthew picked these for ye."

"How is Matthew doing?" Maxi opened the door wider. "Come in, Daniel." Daniel hesitated. "Are ye sure?"

"Yes, very sure." Maxi limped back two steps.

Daniel entered, nodding to Tabby and the young woman standing next to her. The young woman resembled Maxi in her eyes and smile. "Good Morn, Ms. Tabby and Ma'am."

"Good Morn Daniel," Tabby replied. "This is Aprell, Maxi's granddaughter."

"Just as lovely as her granny." Daniel faced Aprell. "Pleasure to greet ya, young lady."

"Same here, Mr. Yost." Aprell reached for the bouquet. "I can put those in a vase and water."

"Thank ye." Daniel let go of the bouquet and set the basket of apples and peaches on the counter. "Matthew is fine. His scraped knee is healing fine. He sends his apologies for not thinking about the blasted sidewalk tilt."

Maxi smirked. "Daniel, Matthew isn't responsible for the sidewalk. None of us are. I should have known better."

"Ah, darlin', we're young at heart." Daniel winked and added, "Even if the flesh don't agree."

Maxi smiled and ducked her head. Daniel reached out, laid his hand on Maxi's cast, and continued speaking. "May your injuries heal fast and well. May your heart be young and your spirit understand the limitations of the flesh. That said, I got a question for ya."

Aprell filled the vase she found in the glassware cabinet with water and put the bouquet in it. She set the vase and bouquet on the table. She nudged Tabby and nodded toward the kitchen entryway. Tabby nodded. They quickly exited the kitchen.

Daniel pulled out a chair from the table. He patted the chair. "Please sit with me for a moment."

Maxi sat down. Daniel pulled out the chair next to Maxi and sat in it. He clasped Maxi's uncasted hand. "May I continue with me question?"

"Yes." Maxi's gaze met his.

"Will ye do me an honor of having dinner with me Friday eve?" Daniel raised Maxi's hand, kissed the back of it and let go. "Home-cooked meal at my residence. Chaperoned or unchaperoned."

"Daniel, are you asking me out?" Maxi glanced toward the kitchen entrance. Tabby and Aprell weren't in sight. She was alone with Daniel Yost. Daniel, the one that set her to sighing and—Maxi pinched her leg through her jeans. Jeans that she'd taken to wearing at the advice of Kenneth Maxwell, orthopedist extraordinaire. Keep her legs warmer, no panty hose chafing her legs or scrapes, and easier to get on by herself. Mom jeans as Kenneth called them. Elastic waist, no belt needed. And long-sleeved knit pullover tops. Changes from dresses or skirts and low heels. Change from one decade to another within hours. Ordinary mortal actions felt like magic speeded up. No wonder mortals often looked at magics in dismay.

"Aye, Maxi, darlin'." Daniel winked and continued speaking. "Asking, wanting time with ye. If we must be chaperoned, please choose one that will not blush and fuss when I hugs and kisses ya."

Maxi tittered and ducked her head. She fanned herself, leaned closer to Daniel and whispered, "I think we're alone now. How about we practice the kissing part?"

Daniel glanced behind him and around the kitchen twice. He scooted the chair closer to her, his lips puckered, and. . .

Aprell motioned Tia Tabby closer. "Grandmother and Mr. Yost are . . ."

Tabby nudged Aprell. "Step away if you're embarrassed. No different than when you and Evan were kissing and hugging."

"*You watched us?*" Aprell faced Tia Tabby.

"No, checked on you." Tabby smiled and added, "Donya and Maxi watched and took side bets on how long each kiss would last."

"*TIA TABBY!*" Aprell wondered why the room was suddenly very warm. "Bets? Please, none of you were magicing Evan and me, were you?'

"*Shhhh!*" Tia Tabby put a finger to her lips and nodded toward the kitchen. "Witch's oath to the One. Not a spark or sputter of magic from any of us."

"You mean like the magic that's happening between Mr. Yost and Grandmother, it happened with Evan and me?" Aprell pressed her lips together. Her and Evan, their own magic? Natural attraction? Was that what she inhaled and drew deep into her inner core? Evan's pheromones, his natural scent mixed with his Mixed Spice soap and aftershave? The scents that lulled her to sleep that night? That stayed with her for several days as if Evan marked her?

Tia Tabby nodded. "We'll talk about that soon. Right now. Daniel and Maxi need a bit more privacy."

Tabby motioned Aprell away from the kitchen doorway. Out of the corner of her eye, she caught Daniel and Maxi moving closer to each other.

Daniel's lips met Maxi's. A soft brush, followed by a firmer second kiss, followed by another with lips parted. Maxi leaned tighter to Daniel. Her hand slid up Daniel's arm, stopping at his shoulder. The tip of Daniel's tongue brushed against hers and pulled back. His hands clasped her arms, holding her firmly, and steadying her. He parted his lips more. His tongue ventured forward, teasing hers, seeking entrance. The age-old mating dance began. Tongues tasting, sipping and savoring the essence of each as they retreated.

Daniel slowly pulled back, pressing his lips against Maxi's once more, and slid his hands down her arms. He righted Maxi and moved upright. "Darlin' good thing no smoke alarms went off."

Maxi smirked and shook her finger at him. "No problem with setting them off. Of course, the kitchen one needs a new battery."

"New battery taken care of, darlin', if ye got one." Daniel stood. "And a steady stool or ladder to stand on."

"Battery is in the drawer near the door. Steady step ladder I got." Maxi rose and walked to the kitchen doorway. "Tabby, can you get the step ladder out of the hall closet, please?"

"Sure Maxi. One moment." Tabby got the step ladder from the closet and handed it to Daniel.

Daniel took the step ladder from Tabby, got the battery out of the drawer and changed the smoke detector's battery. "Need my darlin' Maxi and family safe."

"Thank you, Daniel." Maxi snuggled closer to Daniel as he leaned against the counter. "Dinner at your place sounds wonderful. What time?"

"Sevenish. I'll be in touch to find out if ye are chaperoned or not for a head count of how many I cook for." Daniel brushed his lips over hers again, opened the door, and exited whistling a jaunty tune as he went down the steps, making his way through the backyard toward the gateway onto Main Street.

Quiet flooded the kitchen. Maxi stood gazing at Daniel sauntering down Main Street, waving at people, stopping to speak with a few. Her last view of him was him turning, waving and crossing the street before the corner tree lawn blocked her view. Maxi sighed, closed the door with a heavy thud, and walked back to her chair.

Maxi gently sat down. She had a date Friday night. A date with Daniel Yost. Daniel Yost whose hugs and kisses ignited sparks and sputters like her ex-husband Joshua did when they first started courting. Six years into the marriage, three children and a mutual agreement that marriage wasn't their thing, they amicably split up. Joshua kept their friendship alive until he passed. Maxi let out a low sob, wiped a tear off her cheek and rose.

Aprell rushed into the kitchen. "Grandmother, are you okay?"

"Yes, Aprell. Brief stroll down memory lane." Maxi pulled a napkin out of the napkin holder on the table. She blotted her face and faced Aprell. "I've taken time to mourn, to heal and to be overly cautious."

"Overly cautious?" Aprell handed her grandmother a glass of water.

"Yes, guarding my heart. Keeping me safe from heartbreak and loneliness, I thought." Maxi drank part of the water and set the glass down. "What I really accomplished was a different kind of loneliness. The kind where you risk following your heart. Taking a risk on the attraction you feel."

Aprell sat in the chair next to her grandmother. "Could you please explain more?"

"Aprell, your grandfather and I stayed good friends after our amicable split up. Joshua went on to find love and remarried. His family embraced your mother, your aunts and I as part of their tribe." Maxi drank more of the water. "Joshua encouraged me to find another partner. A new boyfriend. I resisted not because I wanted Joshua back. I resisted out of fear. Fear that I'd make the same wrong mistake again. Don't you and Evan make the same mistake. Follow your hearts. Go for what you want."

Aprell hugged her grandmother and kissed her cheek. "Evan and I will find our way on our own terms. No magic necessary, okay?"

"Witch's Oath, no magic unless asked." Maxi smiled. "Send Tabby in, please. I've got some questions for her."

Aprell filled her tea mug, got her ham cheese sandwich out of the microwave and exited the kitchen. Second chances were unplanned. Unplanned happenings at moments when they were least expected. Maybe that was what was happening for her and Evan. Looked like it was happening for her grandmother as well.

"Tia Tabby, Grandmother wants to talk with you." Aprell continued down the hall to her room. She had twenty minutes before her videoconference call with Nancy. After that, she had two back-to-back client sessions. Time to sort out her feelings and jot a few notes about what she was feeling about Evan might be possible.

Tabby entered the kitchen. "Aprell said you want to talk."

Maxi patted the chair next to her. "Yeah. Got a couple of things I need to sort out. I'd ask you and Donya. She isn't here. So it's you and me."

Tabby sat next to Maxi. "What's up? You having second thoughts about Daniel?"

"Not second or third. First thoughts. Memory lane blips of Joshua and I." Maxi drummed her fingers on the table. "Daniel asked me to dinner Friday night. He said chaperoned or unchaperoned."

"You're having second thoughts about this?" Tabby leaned forward, laid her hand on Maxi's and added, "Let me correct that and ask you letting your and Joshua's blunder mar your thoughts?"

"Not spoil. Reminder of why I haven't dated or sought anyone's company other than those I implicitly trust. You and Donya." Maxi slid her hand out from under Tabby's

"Trust and fear. I get it." Tabby nodded. "Been there. Hard to let go of the what-if worst-case scenario."

"You're going with me Friday night." Maxi rose and pushed her chair to the table.

"*I'm what?*" Tabby bolted out of the chair. She rocked back on her heels and grabbed the table, steadying herself to keep from wobbling. A loud clatter and bang sounded as the chair hit the floor.

"Chaperoning Daniel and me Friday night. You're available, right?" Maxi grinned flipping up the weekly wall calendar she kept near the stove. "That's four days from now. Oh, yeah. You can bring a date."

"Maxi Waller, are you insinuating I need a date to chaperone you and Daniel? You and Daniel need chaperones?" Tabby started pacing, walking around the fallen chair as she looped around the table on her first lap.

Maxi snapped her fingers and pointed at Tabby. "Maybe you need a chaperone. Say Daniel and I chaperone you and—I know who you can get."

Tabby stopped mid-lap. She rolled her eyes and asked, "Dare I ask who?"

Maxi, grinning and nodding, replied, "Mario Gomez."

"*Mario?*" Tabby continued her lap. "What makes you think Mario wants to go out with me?"

"Come on, Tabby. You and Donya set it up for dinner delivery the night Aprell arrived. You can cash in the rain check Mario offered you when you said you weren't sure when you were available." Maxi stepped in front of Tabby.

Tabby sidestepped. Maxi copied Tabby's move, keeping her in front of her. Tabby heaved a deep sigh, reached down, picked up the chair and shoved it against the table. The table vibrated some. Maxi steadied the chair. "Tabby, what's got you so agitated?"

Tabby looked down and back up. "Do you know how long it's been since I dated?"

Maxi burst out laughing. "Probably as long as me or Donya. We looked, did not touch or ask. Gotta get back in practice. Friday is the start!"

Tabby groaned, shrugged and threw up her hands. "Okay! Okay! I'll talk to Mario tomorrow."

Maxi picked up the kitchen phone handset and held it out. "Why not right now?"

CHAPTER TEN

Aprell finished her sandwich, wiped her hands and ended her videoconference call with Nancy. Charms and Spells was set to have a high-profit month. Nancy had hired an assistant to oversee the shop while she was out calling on clients or doing in-office visits with medical professionals. Alternative medicine was gaining popularity, and more people were accessing the shop's website. Nancy's suggestion of opening a shop in Sylvan Valley caught Aprell off guard. Nancy explained that with one of them in an established human, magic and supernatural mixed community, more acceptance and visibility would result. Updating the website and SEO terms would be needed. Aprell wrapped her hands around her tea mug letting the remaining warmth seep into her hands. Expansion was something she and Nancy discussed on a regular basis. The expansion was in Hawaii, not elsewhere. Was this a signal? A nudge from the powers-that-be that change was happening in a direction she hadn't consciously considered? Perhaps completely accepted?

Aprell glanced at the notes she'd jotted during her two client sessions. Each wanted something. Each needed tangible proof things were happening. Crystal magic worked to a point. Getting either of her clients to understand they needed to embrace their own internal magic was the hard part. A demi-witch of mixed heritage wanted to understand her magic. That wasn't something crystal magic could answer. Healing and acceptance of who, what, and how the demi-witch went about this was something she had to do on her own. Seeking out a referral to a magic or supernatural mental health practitioner in Hawaii Nancy offered to take on. The other client had asked for local references to a magical physician. Again Nancy had taken the search request on and would be following up with both clients. Aprell downed the last of her barely warm tea. Was this another sign she wasn't needed in Hawaii any longer? Aprell let go a long, deep sigh and pulled her personal journal to her. She opened to her last entry a week prior as she sat waiting for the taxi to take her to the airport.

I'm heading back. Back to where I came from. Is it home? Or is it used to be home? Hawaii is starting to feel like a place I belong. Took time to do that. Moving from island to island, apartment to apartment didn't help. Who am I? A crystal magician. Crystal healer and . . .there's more I can feel. Putting it into words isn't easy. I feel as if I've turned a corner. Closed a door while opening another door. Chapter finished, finessed and ready to file in been there, done that and now time to move forward. No looking back. Yet, I must. To understand and learn is to grasp why. I swear a voice whispered in my ear, there's no movement looking back. Looking forward and stepping into the new is movement. I'm getting on the plane. The announcement to board is happening. I'm stepping into the unknown. Sure of one thing, I'm strong, capable and will welcome what the future is showing even if there are still so many questions left unanswered.

Aprell picked up her pen and started writing the next entry.

A week later, I'm still unsure of many things. I'm back—ten years back it feels like at times. Evan and I are interacting with each other. We're igniting sparks and aura blasts like before. Except. . . I stepped out of the back reflection and stroll down memory lane to be in the here and now. Evan and I are not sophomores in high school trying to reignite a floundering relationship attempt. We don't have fledging magics, apprentice matchmakers and supernaturals all going through magic puberty spurts and supernatural morphing. Touching Evan felt very different. There was heat like before, yet the intensity wasn't exploding. It happened naturally. We weren't glancing over our shoulders or around us wondering if we'd been magiced or were under magic's influence. We touched. We kissed. Tia Tabby and Grandmother swore by witch's honor oath no magicing on their part happened either. I don't know what Evan thinks or feels about this beyond the momentary acknowledgment of what we felt. Questions still abound. Has he thought about this? Talked with Tia Donya? Are we really magic-free this time? No other influences except our own internal heart magic happening. Does Evan have that trait?

Evan yawned and stretched. He rubbed his forehead. Two twelve-hour shifts two days in a row were taking their toll. Dr. Hauser's patients were slowly recovering. Instilling confidence in the young shapeshifters was Dr. Hauser's forte. The teens needed a magical physician moving forward. Traditional human medicine was healing the bruises and scrapes both teens had from their first wild hunt and full moon morphing. Evan chuckled as he went back over Dr. Hauser's briefing. Both teens wore glasses in their human form. Tossing their glasses aside and taking off through the dark woods before the moon completed its rise had started the trips, lumps and bumps incidents. Neither teen had listened to their parents and pack alpha briefings. Wild hunts happened in packs for a reason. Making sure they could see and use their heightened senses before leaping into the unknown mattered. Oh, did he know that firsthand. Learning how to shield and defend against magic from a mortal perspective took straddling an invisible fence that loved to reach up, pinch and pull you back down to sit on the splinters waiting to poke your posterior. Ass, arse or whatever you decided to call it.

Evan reached for his cell phone. It had rung twice as he entered chart notes and updated entries for future medicine and treatment that Dr. Hauser would administer. Teaming up with Dr. Hauser and his staff was exhilarating and inclusive. None of the magical physicians had scoffed or dismissed what he said or prescribed. Each asked his opinion and expertise on the human half that other shapeshifters needed help with. Even two supernatural medical doctors stopped him in the hospital hall asking if they could talk with him about his uncanny ability to sense what his patients needed. One mentioned his personal magic might be a bit extrasensory in nature. Evan shook his head. He needed to talk with Abada about this once he got back to Sylvan Valley.

Evan glanced at the caller ID. The last call was from Abada. He'd call her in a moment after he checked the two text messages showing. Both displayed Aprell's number. He opened the first, smiling and laughing as he read the message twice:

Hope you're well. Busy here. Grandmother has a date! She's singing and humming. Tia Tabby and Mr. Gomez are chaperoning Mr. Yost and Grandmother Friday night! Maybe we should go along and make sure everyone behaves. Wait, who's chaperoning who?

Evan read the second message, nodding as he closed the text. Tia Maxi had made it around the block twice without stumbling. She'd taken Tia Tabby up on her offer to go shopping for a new date outfit. Kenneth Maxwell's email confirmed Tia Maxi's scrapes and bruises were healing. Her fractures were barely visible on the x-ray. Keeping the cast on and letting nature do its healing part was Kenneth's continued prognosis. Maxi had kept her acupuncture appointments with Dr. Kwang. He referred her to a massage and physical therapist once the cast was removed in about four weeks at the earliest.

Evan saved the chart file he finished, exited the hospital patient system and sent an email to Dr. Hauser briefing him on how to reach out as needed with questions or concerns. Time had come to go home. Home to what was possibly the next chapter in his life. A chapter that included Aprell. Long distance relationships were hellish from what a few of the residents shared at a colleague dinner social given in his honor three nights ago. How attached was Aprell to Hawaii? Had it become her home? Was he willing to move? Relocate and reestablish his practice? Questions that they both had to answer. Neither of their feelings was above the others.

Evan zipped his jacket closed, shut off his laptop, and put it in his backpack. He'd pack up the rest of his stuff in the morning. A quick shower, a bit to eat and eight hours solid sleep were the last items on his to-do list after he called Abada.

Twenty minutes later, Evan stuffed the trash from his take-out meal in the wastebasket close to the hotel room door. He tossed his clothes on the bed as he shucked them. A quick shower was next. He adjusted the water temperature, stepped under the spray and soaped down. He deleted three text messages he started to Aprell. Every one of them was full of questions. Things that text messages weren't going to answer. Discussions that needed face-to-face settings. Settings with only he and Aprell present.

Aprell had asked about his day. He sent an email without many details. HIPPA kept him from saying a lot. There was something he wanted to ask her that went along with the discussion questions for the face-to-face setting. The teen shapeshifters' pack spiritual leader had mentioned candle magic and crystal healing twice as Dr. Hauser talked with the family and the spiritual leader. Candle magic Evan understood to a point. Meditation and focusing on healing were essential parts of alternative medicine he participated in during his residency in Chicago at the human hospital.

Meditating focused on the present here and now worked for him at various times. Like trying to sleep when his mind refused to gear down and slumber. Learning how to visualize the lit candle in his mind and focus on the light helped send signals to his subconscious and conscious mind. The two merged together like they spoke, agreeing that running helter-skelter chasing impulses and jambled thoughts wasn't refreshing. The one thing that still ignited his occasional chuckle on the nights he used the visual to relax into sleep was one part of his mind flashing images, trying to recapture his attention.

Flashes of past sexual encounters and so-called conquests cropped up from time to time. Conquests were one-sided too often for him. He wanted someone to connect with, share ideas and discussions, find a common bond that resonated outside of a sexual olympics spark and fizzle out. He wanted a relationship. Someone who got him. Understood him without his needing to overly explain. That came with dating, sharing and discussing their beliefs, ethics and mores. One person captured his attention in that way. Aprell fit that in so many ways. His other close fits had dissolved when he started asking questions about magic and attempting to understand. Abada had held him and shared his frustrations and tears concerning that.

Evan ducked under the shower spray, rinsed, and shampooed his hair. One consistent thought filled his mind as he rinsed off again, taking much of his focus. Could he and Aprell connect this time in a way that left them solidly feeling their chemistry and magic? No other magic was mixed in. He shut the shower off, quickly toweled off and hung the towel on the rack on the back of the bathroom door. He had a few questions for Abada before he talked with Aprell and drifted into slumber, dreaming of being home. Home where he and Aprell connected, pursued and decided on their relationship status. Their personal magic connection would be enough. Beyond that, no magic necessary.

He pulled on his sleep shorts and crawled under the covers. His cell phone beside him. He scrolled through his contacts. Stopped at Abada's number and hit the call button. The next few moments would either solidify his plan or add to his growing list of questions.

"Hello, Evan," Abada answered on the third ring.

"Were you sitting on your phone?" Evan chuckled. The joke started in his junior year of high school with his first flip cell phone. Silencing the ringer and buzzer plus stashing it in his hip pocket was the only way he could keep his phone with him. One time he forgot to turn the ringer on after he got home from school. He missed Abada's calls and text message alerts. Only way he found out she'd been trying to reach him while at the market was when she got home.

"Not on it. By it, yes. Too large to fit in my hip pocket." Abada's laughter joined his. "How are things going?"

"I released my patients to Dr. Hauser. Quite a few magical physicians have asked about referrals. Partnering is happening in ways I didn't think could." Evan yawned and stretched. "I've got a few questions."

"Okay." Donya yawned. "That is catchy."

Evan yawned again. "Sorry, two twelve-hour days back to back. Tires even the healthiest physician out."

"Want to wait on your questions?"

"No, need some answers." Evan stuffed a pillow behind him. "I want an honest answer. I know you won't lie to me."

"Correct. You and I agreed no lies between us from the time you came to live with grandfather and me. Ask away. I'll answer as best I can."

"I'm asking this cuz I need to hear it. You, Tia Tabby and Tia Maxi haven't magiced Aprell or me, right?" Evan held his phone tighter to his ear.

Abada's sigh brushed his ear as she replied. "Sigh is because we didn't teach you and Aprell how to shield when you were younger. No, no magic from any of us. Why do you ask?"

"Sparks. Colors I don't normally see. Feelings that blow through me and echo when Aprell and I are together. One thought keeps coming up every time I think about what's happening."

"What is that?"

"Heart Magic. Those words that get blasted around near Valentine's Day. Or Cauldron Falls or Sylvan Valley Sadie Hawkins events."

"Heart magic exists. It's a separate magic. A natural magic that pulsates and is born when two people connect. You feel and know. Remember when I taught you about meditation and listening to your inner voice?"

Evan shifted lower in the bed. "Yeah. I been doing that to disconnect from the noise around me to sleep or cat nap this week. Weird dreams some nights. Unclear images with words popping up."

Donya tittered. "Evan, you have your own magic. Humans don't recognize their magic because it's not part of their natural evolution. Your magic is understanding what your patients need and reading their silent non-verbal messages. You pick up on this."

"Are you saying I've got magic?"

"Human natural magic, yes. Heart magic happening? Possibly. That is for you and Aprell to decide. As to your doctor magic, your mother said one of your great-grandaunts on your father's side possessed an uncanny knack for reading people and situations. Some say it might be extrasensory perception. Second sight. Either way, don't worry."

"Abada, te quiero. Thanks for answering my questions. Reminding me to listen to my inner voice and connect with my heart. The gifts you, Grandfather, Momma and Dad gave me as part of my creation." Evan yawned again. "Good night, Abada. I'll be home tomorrow. We'll talk about Tia Maxi's date then."

"Good night, Evan. Te quiero tambien."

Donya glanced at her watch. Ten PM wasn't too late to call her coven sisters and find out what they'd been stirring up.

Tabby answered on the fourth ring. "Donya, why are you calling this late?"

"Not late by our usual standards. Unless you are starting to keep old folks hours?" Donya grinned as Tabby sputtered and fussed.

"I'm not old. I'm in the prime of my middle-witch second century, thank you." Tabby blew a raspberry in the phone twice.

Donya burst out laughing. "What have you and Maxi been up to? Conjuring dates? Love potions again?"

CHAPTER ELEVEN

Tabby held her phone away from her ear. Donya sounded jealous? Teasing? Tabby put her phone back to her ear. "Why would I let Maxi conjure or make love potions? You and I agreed she needed to stop doing both."

"I hear you got hot dates for Friday night." Donya's tone was light and upbeat.

Tabby shook her head. Had Maxi called Donya? Donya called Maxi?

"Donya, let's cut the chase as Evan says. Who told you and what did they tell you?" Tabby put her phone on speaker and set it on the bedside nightstand.

Donya's titter rushed out of the speaker. "Tabby, mutual connection. Evan and Aprell. You are extended family so you're looped in."

Tabby rolled her eyes. Evan and Aprell the two foundational bricks in the upcoming Friday night dinner date chaperone contest. Who was chaperoning and who was dating she wasn't sure. Now Donya wanted in on things?

Tabby rolled on her side, propping herself up on her pillows. "Donya, Mr. Yost came over, checked on Maxi and asked her to dinner at his house. He's mentioned chaperones or not."

"Tabby, you going alone?" Donya didn't say more.

Tabby gripped the edge of the blanket covering her. Al lay close by washing all his fur and other cat areas. He glanced up at her, blinked, flicked his tail and started washing where a specific part of his anatomy used to be. Al looked up at her again, hissed and jumped down off the bed.

Tabby glared at Al as his cat arse sauntered out of the bedroom. Familiars were supposed to be helpful. Not royal pains in the—Donya repeated her questions. "Tabby, cat got your tongue? Al being obnoxious? Do you have a date with Mario Gomez Friday night?"

"Donya, you jealous? Want to come along?" Tabby let go of the blanket. Which one of them would go for the next upwitchship jab?

"Depends." Donya paused for several moments. Tabby reached for the phone when Donya blurted out. "Maybe Aprell and Evan are chaperoning you and Mario, Maxi and Daniel and me and. . ."

Tabby grabbed her phone and sat up. "Who's conjuring dates and love potions now?"

"No one. I was thinking who I might like to have a home-cooked meal with." Donya started humming, snapped her fingers and continued, "Raphael Gutierrez. Best short order cook in Cauldron Falls."

"Raphael?" Tabby groaned. "He regularly burns pancakes, sets off the smoke detector and overcharges for everything."

Donya's laughter blasted out of the phone speaker. "Seriously, Tabby, I know not to let Raphael near my kitchen, your kitchen or any kitchen. That's why he relocated to Cauldron Falls."

"You going solo then?" Tabby reached out toward Al as he jumped back up on the bed, settling close to her.

"Not solo. Lucian Chargena has asked me out a couple of times. He's a great conversationalist. Cooks divine Tex-Mex cuisine. Three men cooking for us. Makes a grand date, don't you think?"

"What about Aprell and Evan?" Tabby stroked Al's fur. Al started purring.

"Oh yeah. Our chaperones for the evening. What do you think we should do with them while the six of us play Spin-the-Bottle after dinner? Or a rousing game of strip poker?"

Tabby opened her mouth, closed it and tried to speak. Words wouldn't form. Had Donya been doing fertility incantations again? "Str-strip poker? You mean get naked?"

"Well, yeah. That's what happens when you play strip poker. Unless we all start out naked and put clothes on as we lose." Donya didn't say more.

"Donya Marianna Alvarez, have you been taste-testing potions again? Mixing decanting and spell incantations?" Tabby clicked the speaker off and held the phone to her ear.

"No, Tabby Lucia Nichols. I ain't, haven't and know blessedly better than that. I'm not a novice enchantress or potion brewer. You forget this? Old age catching up with you?' Donya's laughter roared out of the phone.

Tabby shook her head and grinned. "Gotcha banter on both our parts?"

Donya's breathy laughter softened. "Yup. I guess we're doing a group double date Friday night. Evan's due back tomorrow. Let me talk with him and see what his schedule looks like for a confab before Friday night."

"Sounds good, Donya. Sleep well. Pleasant dreams." Tabby started to lower her phone.

"Hey Tabby, don't let your dreams conjure up too many naked men. You might not want to get up when Al wakes you up in the morning." Donya's good night and laughter continued as she ended the call.

Tabby laid her phone on the nightstand. She glanced at Al as he fluffed the section of the comforter he laid on and mewed. "Al, you keep your thoughts to yourself. If I want to dream about naked men my age, thank you, I will. My dreams are not yours to police or wander through. Got it?"

Al flashed her a cat cheesy hissy grin and closed his eyes. Tabby petted Al one last time, turned on her side, turned off the lamp and settled beneath her covers. She hoped Donya's suggestion populated her dreams. Tomorrow they could compare what male anatomy they managed to dream up and how many times they accomplished the task successfully.

Donya set the alarm on her cell phone for ten a.m. She'd probably be awake before then. Evan would stop by before he headed on to his place. He might even stay a day or two since she was closer to the hospital than his place. Maybe they could cook breakfast together like they used to before he moved to New York for medical school. She missed having him around. Missed having someone around. Taking in a roommate or housemate didn't pulsate with her. Having a friend or family member living with her offered companionship and opportunities for shared experiences. Too bad her, Maxi, and Tabby's couple of attempts had petered out.

Donya laid her cell phone on the nightstand, turned off the light, and snuggled the covers around her. As her eyes drifted closed, two brief images flashed through her mind. Image of Errol blowing her a kiss good night and an image of Lucian grinning and nodding his head. Oh Luna, were the two of them matchmaking her. "Errol," she sleepily murmured, "Behave. I can't matchmake and magic. Neither can you."

But, my love, you shouldn't be alone. Lucian and you need each other.

"Errol, describe need. If you can't, then let me sleep. Lucian and I can figure this out on our own."

Errol's laughter brushed over her cheek and ear. Donya reached up, patting what others would say was air. To her and Errol, she patted his cheek and blew him a sleepy airborne kiss.

Evan rolled over and shut his alarm off. Odd dreams and scenes scattered throughout his sleep. Bits and pieces of his grandfather Errol advising him on heart magic. Spurts of memories from his and Aprell's earlier attempts at a relationship and friendship. Abada popped in there a couple of times. Evan smiled as he sat up.

Abada and Grandfather scolding each other about finding out if he had magic. Even a tiny, itty bitty drop or spatter. Some would dismiss the odd dreams and scenes as sleep time brain attempts at making sense out of his awake thoughts and info over the last week. Info he was still sorting through and trying to make cohere together. At one point, two echoes whispered through his semialert moments as he used the bathroom. Their refrain of it doesn't have to make sense now made him grin again. Reminded him of his first med school class on observation and quantifying info. Gather data, measure similarities, and look for like groups. That was where his thoughts meshed into a partial understanding. Acceptance by other physicians and medical personnel, magical or non-magical, came with time. Now might be the time for his acceptance and understanding of how they could partner in healing humans, supernaturals, and magics.

He shucked his sleep shorts, tossed them on top of his closed suitcase and turned on the shower. In amongst his three a.m. thoughts, flashes of his teenage fantasies clamored for time and space. Space to trickle tendrils of desire and intrigue deep into his core. Deeper into his nether region until his cock and balls swelled, demanding attention and relief. Rolling over on his stomach had silenced their plea demands and allowed him to drift back off. His dreams had taken a different approach.

Close to the middle of their senior year, he and Aprell had snuck out wanting time to sort out who they were as a couple and individuals. Three couples had caught up with them and an impromptu game of strip spin-the-bottle had the eight of them buckass naked under the full moon overhead and the light from the fire pit. He memorized Aprell's illumination with a thirst that the others didn't detonate. Each of the other women were yummy to look at. He'd given them hot ogling once-overs before the game ended. The dudes danced around showing off their cocks and balls. Everyone present got fondles and copped feels in.

Evan stepped into the shower. Water sluiced down over him. Warmth mixed with blasts of cooler water spilled out of the shower as he adjusted the temperature. He soaped and rinsed the upper half of his body. His erection stared back at him as he relathered his hands. Time to seek the relief both wanted. He slid his soap-slicked hands down and over him until he reached his balls. Evan reached between his legs, cupping his balls. Slow strokes up and down, squeezing on the upward strokes as he reached the top of his cock. Over and across his glans and back down to where his hand held his balls. Faster upward strokes, lightly squeezing his glans as he reached it. Pre-come oozed out, slicking his fingers and glans. Evan worked the fluid over him with his palm and fingers. He picked up pace, thrusting through his slicked partially closed fist. Sliding into Aprell, holding her close, suckling her nipples, and rubbing her clitoris in between thrusts. One more stroke and—Evan captured his bottom lip between his teeth, muffling part of his deep low groan. Semen squirted out, coating more of his hand and fingers. The coating drizzled off him as he stepped under the shower spray. He resoaped his hands and worked the suds over his cock and balls. He rinsed and turned the shower off.

Twenty minutes later, Evan loaded his backpack and suitcase into his car. He looked up, pointed toward the cloud directly overhead, grinned and formed the okay symbol with his thumb and forefinger. As if the heavens, his grandfather, Luna and the One responded in unison, the cloud moved enough to let a sunbeam shine down almost exactly where he stood. As he pulled out of the hotel's parking lot, he knew two things. He and Aprell were experiencing a connection that they'd missed before or weren't ready for. The other thing was change was happening for them and their families. Who, what, where, when and how were unknown.

Evan dialed in Cauldron Falls and Sylvan Valley's joint oldies but goodies radio station as he turned onto the highway leading back to Sylvan Valley. Oldie love songs topped the hour. He chuckled as he finished singing along with two of the songs, glad no one was within earshot. As the last song faded, Evan glanced at the dashboard clock. Was eight-thirty a.m. too early to call Aprell?

Aprell sat on the side of her bed. Twice during the night, Evan entered her dreams. Dreams that had the two of them nude and ogling each other. In the one dream, their mirrored reflections showed their younger teenage faces. The age they'd first held hands, experimentally kissed and hugged. Sex was not on their agenda until they found themselves alone. Alone, unchaperoned and ready to follow their hormonal-driven urges to an end that didn't happen. Not because they were interrupted. A blasted four-legged feline chaperone decided screwing the neighbor's inheat female cat outside the bedroom window. Yowls, howls, hisses and spatting might have turned Al and his conquests on. Al and his ladies' serenade had stopped her and Evan faster than if someone had doused them with a couple buckets of ice water. Her last dream roused her. Need and desire raced through her igniting an urge that masturbating hadn't cooled much. Could she and Evan do it to get the physical hormones under control enough to discuss what came next?

A knock on her bedroom door roused her from her thoughts. Aprell rose, pulling on her robe as she made her way to the door. "One moment, please."

She opened the door, stepped back and started to shove the door shut. What was Evan doing standing outside her bedroom door at ten a.m.? He wasn't due back until late afternoon.

"Hold on, Aprell," Evan stated, stopping the door with his hand. "I'm back early."

"Yeah, and got everyone in the house wondering what we're doing in here." Aprell peered around the door. "Could you wait until I'm dressed, and we talk in the living room?"

"Tia Maxi and Tia Tabby are walking with Mr. Yost and Mr. Gomez. They headed toward the park." Evan pushed against the door. "Tia Maxi told me you were in your room. She heard you moving about."

"What if we're caught?" Aprell let go of the door. "I am not doing a witch shotgun wedding nor any fake engagement!"

Evan laughed pushing the door wide open. He leaned against the door frame, crossed his arms over his chest, and grinned. "I'm not either of those, too."

"What do you want then?" Aprell backed away from Evan as he stepped into her bedroom.

"Two things." Evan held up two fingers. "First, let you know I'm back. Two, take you on a breakfast picnic where we can talk without ears."

"Ears aren't here." Aprell shook her head and smiled. "I see you're back. Please go wait in the living room while I grab a shower and dress, okay?"

Evan nodded, blew her a kiss and exited her bedroom. Aprell leaned out of the bedroom doorway, watched Evan saunter down the hall and into the living room. She shoved the bedroom door closed. Latching it with a loud thud, causing the doorknob to rattle and jangle. Aprell leaned against the door, her hand over her mouth, laughing at her own internal pun. What if the lock stuck again like the other night when she woke up in the middle of the night and tried to sneak out for a snack? It took her and her grandmother twenty minutes to pick the lock open. She promised to not lock the lock again. Damn, Had she done what she promised not to? Had her heart done what her mind kept telling it not to do?

Aprell shucked her robe and nightgown. She trotted to the bathroom, counting her steps, hoping to distract her thoughts. One image kept coming up, making her stop and restart her counting. Evan embracing her as they sat on the wicker bench. His lips meeting hers and one passionate kiss leading to another. Hands roamed a bit. Car horns, car doors opening and shutting kept them from losing themselves in the moment. In the heat of passion that threatened to swamp them in a large pounding wave. No cold shower was going to change what could have happened if they were inside and alone. Sexual pheromones pulsed around them then and might now. Goddess, help them that they could chaperone themselves. They needed the practice if they were going to chaperone her grandmother, Tia Tabby, Tia Donya and their dates. Were any of them capable of effectively chaperoning themselves much less anyone else?

CHAPTER TWELVE

Evan glanced back at the hall as he entered the living room. He'd never seen Aprell so adamant about him leaving her alone. She'd fussed and cussed at him years ago. Walked away. Never hid or talked to him with a curt tone. What had her apprehensive?

He hoped she hadn't clicked the lock. Getting caught trying to pick the bloody damn lock by Tia Maxi and Tia Tabby wasn't something either of them or Abada would let them forget or live down. Evan walked to the couch, drummed his fingers against his leg and shrugged.

Aprell needed space. She could have said so. Reading her actions took focus. Focus he wasn't sure he was aware of. Had he picked up on her energy? Read her emotions? Understanding this uncanny ability he had was unnerving. Where did he get it from? Why was it showing up now? He dropped onto the couch, picked up the newspaper lying next to him and leafed through the pages. Distraction might help him relax.

Aprell tossed the bath sheet on the towel rack and entered her bedroom. Counting the odd colored dots on the shower curtain pattern had worked some. She knew that facing what she felt was one way to get to what was happening. Another way was endless questions. A few answers and quite a bit of supposing. Not good in getting to the heart of the matter. Heart matters. Matters that stumped matchmakers from the first and continuing through their descendants. Had heart magic bounced through her igniting waves of uncertainty?

She quickly dressed. As she tied her sneakers, Aprell repeated two words. Mutual understanding. Evan and she needed to explain their feelings. Discuss what was going on and—two rapid knocks on the bedroom door sounded.

"Aprell, tell me you didn't lock the door."

Had Evan told her grandmother what happened? Had the hard latching of the door rattled the lock in place?

Aprell rose. She grabbed two of the crystals lying next to her crystal pouch and magic book. She palmed the clear quartz and bloodstone, chanting as she moved toward the door.

"Light of energy. Pulse of motion. Move through me and

warm my hands. Direct your flow into the door. Warming and moving that which is cold no more."

Aprell clasped the doorknob with both hands and the crystals. She repeated the chant once more. The doorknob glowed slightly. The glow turned red and yellow, then vanished. Where her fingertips touched, the doorknob grew warm. As she turned the doorknob, a creak and crackle sounded. She opened the door, pulling it toward her. Two pieces of metal fell onto the floor. The outer doorknob hit the floor and rolled toward her.

A gasp sounded. Aprell looked up. Her grandmother, Tia Tabby and Evan stood outside the door staring at her. Evan shrugged and reached for the doorknob.

"Evan, don't touch it for a few moments. Sparks and a flash of reddish glow mean heat. Let the spell dissipate." Maxi moved into the bedroom until she stood next to Aprell. "Your gift is strong. You might want to talk with the Crystal Magic Coven Mistress."

Aprell walked back to the dresser, laid the crystals next to the others on the dresser and faced her grandmother. "Learning how to channel the energy smoother wouldn't hurt. Are there healers among the coven brethren?"

"Yes, there are healers of different persuasions and abilities. The Crystal Coven uses aura energy and kinetic energy as two key elements to their magical talents and traits. Several of our family inherited the trait while others learned how to develop the talent." Maxi pointed to the doorknob, slowly worked her fingers in circular motions clockwise and counterclockwise. "Tabby, please help me cool the metal and focus on chilling the internal parts as well."

Tabby hastily stepped across the dark wooden transition piece indicating the barrier between the bedroom and the hall. Bursts of yellow and red outlined Maxi and reached out toward Aprell. Tabby rolled her shoulders as she inhaled, counting in ancient Latin and in between each number she murmured the connecting spell Maxi sought help with. Disguising their intent, the energy burst reached toward its progenitor, wanting more, wanting to connect and engulf its creator.

Tabby slid her hand along Maxi's cast and wrist, turning her hand as she reached the edges of Maxi's palm. Tabby rubbed her palm across Maxi's until their fingertips touched. Maxi glanced at her. Tabby nodded. In almost perfect unison, they spoke in ancient Latin and Gaelic, pointing their free hands and fingers at the doorknob.

Evan blinked. Shook his head and blinked again. Aprell's hair puffed out like the static electricity experiment they'd done in one of their science classes. If he narrowed his eyes and squinted—no, it couldn't be. He didn't have magic sight. Evan looked away, refocused his view and looked back, squinting again. There it was. A faint yellow and red outline flashed and faded around Aprell. He started to move backwards.

"Evan, stand still. Anyone in the room is an optimal conduit for the energy to pulse towards and overwhelm. Slowly close your eyes and look away. Think of somewhere else you can vividly picture. Don't open your eyes until we say it's okay." Tia Tabby nodded as she spoke.

Evan closed his eyes. Pressed his palms tight against his jeans and legs. Skiing was his passion during high school. His trip to a ski lodge in Colorado had introduced him to snowboarding. Three of his friends and him had raced down the toddler run, ending up on their asses and wiping out until they learned balance. Balance on the white horizon in front of them. The color and cold presented a backdrop that they could call up anytime any of them reminisced about the trip or what they learned.

Shivers ran over his shoulders and down his arms as a key memory played across his mind. Wind blowing snow off the tree limbs as he took the final run the morning of their last day at the resort. He fell flat on his back as the wind picked up. Snow danced around him. Laid on his face and jacket for micro-moments before the wind blew it off him and sent the flakes dancing through the tree line and sky.

"Evan, you can open your eyes," Aprell spoke almost in his ear.

Evan sluggishly left his memory journey, blinking as he opened each eye. He squinted as his vision cleared. Tia Maxi and Tia Tabby faced him.

"What were you thinking about?" Tia Maxi asked, closing the space between them. She held the doorknob between her fingers.

"My junior year Colorado ski trip." Evan pointed at the doorknob. "Safe to hold?"

"Yes, with your help, it is." Tia Tabby laid her hand on his arm. "Your memory vision amplified the cold in the room Maxi, I and Aprell projected. You worked a bit of magic."

Evan shook his head, glanced at Aprell, Tia Tabby and Tia Maxi. "I did what? Remember I'm the non-magical one here."

"I'll put a call into my apartment handyman tomorrow. He's offered to replace the door before. Now is the right time to do it, I'd say." Tia Maxi dropped the doorknob into the wastebasket Aprell held. Tia Maxi patted Evan's shoulder as she moved past him. "Heart magic can ignite things deep within us. Might be your tiny bit of other magic reached out to protect you and those you care about."

"Other magic?" Evan asked, facing Tia Tabby.

"Evan, everyone has a bit of magic in them. Personal magic manifests in different ways for mortals than magics." Tia Maxi paused near him. "Protective magic is a natural part of our survival instinct."

"Self-preservation I get. Seeing auras and sparks?" Evan scowled as he continued. "Either somebody's been holding out on me, or I'm a screwball."

"No one is holding out on you." Aprell patted his shoulder and slid past him out into the hall, heading toward the living room. "Heart magic has me stumped, too. I've read bits and pieces about it. Never anything in depth or studied it."

"Let's reconvene in the living room and get Donya here." Tia Tabby left the hall.

Tia Maxi leaned closer to him, whispering, "Latent traits and talents often manifest with sparks of unknown ignition. Ask Donya about how she found out she could levitate."

Tia Maxi smiled and continued into the living room.

Evan took one step, then another. One foot in front of the other until he was in the living room close to the only open seat. The couch next to Aprell. He squeezed by the coffee table, walked close to Tia Maxi and back around the coffee table. He started to sit as Aprell spoke.

"Evan, sit down. It's all right." Aprell patted the couch. Dust particles danced through the air, swirling and gliding up and down as they caught the sunlight streaming in through the front window. "See nothing unusual."

Evan fished in his jeans pocket, pulled out his cell phone and held it up. "Guess it's time to call Abada."

"Already did." Tia Tabby stood. "Coffee should be done. Anyone else want some breakfast?"

Aprell and Tia Maxi rose. They faced him. "Food, coffee and sweets help when trying to understand the new, unique and mysterious. We've been there. Come on as we try to understand what happened, what is happening and what the bloody dickens heart magic is."

Evan rose and dusted his hands on the seat of his jeans. Damn, he felt like a first-year medical student. Dumb, thought he knew things and figuring out there was a lot he didn't know as many of his first-year professors repeated with each class. Being open to learning, acknowledging he didn't know everything and seeing his supposed teachers scrambling for understanding. Evan chafed his hands. Sometimes, the best learning happened when teachers and students learned together. Okay, he hoped Abada had some understanding to share. All of them finding out together might be unnerving and scary.

Tabby filled three plates with scrambled eggs and sausage patties. As she placed them on the table, she glanced out Maxi's backdoor window. The sun was halfway through the morning sky. Donya said she would make her way over within a half hour. Coffee and a sausage sandwich were her breakfast choices. Two rolls of cinnamon buns were in the oven. Toasted English muffins and homemade peach preserves completed the breakfast. Enough sugar, starch, protein and fiber to keep them going. One end or the other as her grandmere used to joking say.

Aprell took one plate from her and set it in front of Evan. Evan slid the plate in from of Maxi. Tabby plopped the other plate she held onto the empty spot in front of her. "Now look. You've all eaten my cooking before. What's up with you now?"

"I smell manners and caution happening." Aprell pushed back from the table and got four mugs out of the cabinet. "We all were there. We all saw what occurred from our viewpoints. Ain't nothing going to change that."

Maxi took two mugs from Aprell and placed them on the table. "She's right. Unnerving working internmagic like that. Been a long while since I blended my magic with someone else's."

"More like you blended together and the umph pulsed out to all of us. Even me. Damn, I didn't know I had residual magic in me." Evan set his filled mug in front of him and added sugar and cream. He stirred as he continued talking. "Part of me is scolding me for being surprised. I am half mortal and half magical by genetics. Finding out you got bits and scraps of something you never manifested before or could do is like Tia Maxi said damnably unnerving."

Aprell put filled mugs of coffee next to her plate, her grandmother's and Tia Tabby's. "Maybe we need sorta checklist the obvious to clear the clutter from what your mind Evan is trying to make sense of. It'll probably help all of us."

"Evan needs to understand what his mother's magical abilities, talents and traits were." Donya entered the kitchen. "Maxi, you need to latch your porch screen door better. I knocked twice, and it swung open. Good thing I have a key."

"Good thing, I psychically heard you too." Maxi stuck out her tongue and rolled her eyes.

Aprell rapped on the table. "Enough avoiding the obvious invisible elephants, ghostly apparations, and whatever else mortals or magics prefer to call it."

"How about we just call them heebie-jeebies and stop arguing over what to call the issue?" Evan stood, embraced his grandmother and faced the others. "I'm hungry. Getting to hangry. Food first. Second coffee is time enough to learn about what I got, what I ain't got and if my sanity left for the sake of its sanity taking yours along for companionship and their sanities."

Donya quickly set her mug down, covered her mouth, and grabbed her napkin. She wiped her mouth and pointed at Evan. "Pun and innuendos can cease now. We'll talk as we eat. Pausing when any of us has our mugs raised. No spewing coffee at each other. Waste of a damn fine beverage."

Evan saluted her with his mug. He nodded and passed her her sausage sandwich.

Aprell sat down, held up her mug, sipped and set it down with a thud. Everyone looked up. She pointed to each of them as she spoke. "We eat and talk about Friday night group date. Once meal is done and second coffee plus cinnamon rolls are being consumed, we can take up the first two topics again."

Five yeses sounded as the clinking of silverware and plates filled the air.

Tabby wiped her mouth and laid her napkin next to her plate. "Has anyone discussed the group date with Daniel, Mario and Lucian?"

Evan tapped his mug with his spoon. "I think we need a list of who's who to understand the gaggle that's mixing on Friday eve."

Donya chuckled. "Good point, Evan. Lucian is my date."

Evan glanced at her, at Maxi and back to Tabby. "How come no one told me Abada has a date or a boyfriend?"

"Cuz you never asked, Evan." Donya finished her sandwich, wiped her hands and added, "My love life is like you used to tell me when I asked you how much you knew about sex when you hit fifteen. Nada de su negocios. None of your business."

"Touche Abada. Touche." Evan grinned, pointing at her. "Since I'm chaperoning Friday eve, like you used to add, the who, what, where and when info is yours to know and certainly mine to find out."

Aprell handed Evan the last rinsed plate. A fresh pot of coffee was brewing. Tia Tabby had the cinnamon rolls cooling on top of the stove. Breakfast dishes were in the dishwasher. Her grandmother had tossed two legal-sized pads and several pens on the table. Aprell set fresh mugs on the counter along with napkins and dessert plates. From the look of things, this was one of those planning sessions she used to head up for high school dances and events. Could they keep the conversation focused and civil?

CHAPTER THIRTEEN

Donya sat on the couch next to Evan. Tabby and Maxi sat in the wingback chairs facing the couch opposite the coffee table between the chairs and couch. Aprell set the fresh pot of coffee next to the tray of mugs, spoons, creamer, sugar and plate of cinnamon rolls.

"I'm gonna break the ice." Aprell dragged the chair she brought into the living room from the kitchen into the space between the couch and one of the wingback chairs. "Evan will tell his part of it after me to get us on the same page."

"Go ahead, Aprell," Donya said, filling the mugs with coffee.

Aprell glanced at her grandmother and Tia Tabby. Both nodded. Aprell rubbed her hands on her jeans and leaned forward, resting her palms on her knees. "Evan's early arrival caught me off guard. Finding him outside my bedroom door triggered an ingrained response. I wasn't thinking. I reacted instead of acting."

"You caught me off guard, too." Evan took the mug his grandmother handed him. He sipped and nodded. "Thank you, Abada. Just right."

"Welcome, Evan." Donya pointed to the mugs facing Tabby and Maxi. "Go ahead and fix yours while Aprell and Evan continue, please."

Tabby reached for the mug closest to her. "Let me add one thing before Aprell continues. Evan caught all of us off guard with his early arrival."

Maxi added sugar and creamer to her coffee, stirred, sipped and sat back holding her mug. "I think we caught each other off guard. I let him in. Said Aprell was in her room and walked back into my bedroom."

Aprell raised her mug. "Here's to first understanding. We all were on autopilot. Not fully awake."

Evan chuckled. "I claim that. I was in doctor mode and went to your room without thinking that I needed to wait for Tia Maxi or Tia Tabby to let you know I was here."

Donya wet one finger and drew a line in the air. "Confusion and caught off guard one. The rest of you zip. Go on Aprell."

"I shut my bedroom door a bit harder than needed. I didn't think about the lock possibly bumped in place." Aprell sipped more of her coffee and set the mug on the end table close to her. "Figured Evan would go sit down and wait. I showered and dressed. Grandmother's knock on the door jarred my memory about the blasted lock."

Donya turned to Evan. "What happened while Aprell showered and dressed?"

Evan ducked his head. "I came out to the living room, sat down with the paper and started going through it. Tia Maxi came out and asked me if Aprell was still in her room. I said I think so cuz she sorta slammed the door shut."

"I'm going to surmise what happened next." Donya set her mug on the coffee table. "Maxi, you and Tabby plus Evan went to check out where Aprell was. Still in her room and you had to deal with the lock. How did you get the door unlocked?"

Aprell pointed to Evan. "Your turn."

"Evan, did you pick the lock again?" Donya put her hands on her hips.

"I wish that was the easy explanation." Evan stood and started pacing. "I saw auras, sparks and actually felt the magic energy happening. It was like I was part of what was going on."

Donya looked at Maxi. "What?"

Aprell coughed, getting everyone's attention. "Short description. I used crystal magic to heat the lock and open the door. Grandmother, with Tia Tabby's help, cast a cooling spell and douse the heat energy spell I cast. Evan closed his eyes as they directed. His thoughts were so vivid that the energy pulsed out of him and increased the cooling spell."

"Yeah, but how did I do that? How come I saw auras and sparks, Abada? I've never seen them before or even pulsed magic." Evan dropped down on the couch.

Donya tore off a piece of cinnamon roll. Broke it into smaller pieces, laying them on a napkin in her lap. "I'm not sure this is going to make much sense. I'm going to try to explain it from a scientific perspective."

Evan nodded.

Donya held up a small piece of cinnamon roll. "This is a trait. You would call it a gene. Like you got genes from your father and your mother. Each of them makes up part of you."

Evan picked up two of the medium-sized pieces off her lap. "This is the dominant genes I got from my father. The reason I'm nonmagical, right?"

Donya nodded. "Your father's genes are your dominant ones. But. . ." Donya paused.

Evan grinned and vigorously nodded. "Parts of mother are still there. Something ignited those parts to activate. Okay, I get that. Am I a halfie as a lot of people refer to hybrids?"

Maxi tapped on the end table with her mug as she set it down. "You're Evan. You've gained your place and community respect. Remember Tabby and I said everyone even mortals have a bit of magic in them?"

Aprell walked over to the arm of the couch and perched on it next to Evan. "My parents were mixed magics. Crystal magic and witch spell casting. I got the crystal magic dominant gene. Remember how it took me until I started having periods before I could cast simple spells easily? It's like the latent human gene from way back needed to spark something."

"Gene stuff I get. You all mentioned heart magic. What's that? Where'd I get it from?" Evan popped the cinnamon roll bits he held in his mouth and chewed.

Donya sipped more of her coffee. She glanced at Tabby and Maxi, then Aprell. None of them were licensed matchmakers. They did the occasional love potion, tarot card love spread and introduced a few lonely hearts. Heart magic wasn't that simple, easy-peasy explanation.

Tabby walked into the kitchen and retrieved the pads and pens off the table. She held one out to Evan, Donya and Maxi. She tore sheets off each one as she handed out the pads. "Ven diagram is the best way I know how to explain the basics. Draw two intersecting circles. Where the circles intersect, draw a heart."

Each drew the circles and heart. Evan looked up first. "Heart magic is where the intersection happens?"

"More than that," Tabby replied. "It's where two hearts intersect. Like your parents love. Donya and Errol's love. Maxi's love with Joshua. Aprell's parents love. And mine with my late husband."

"When two hearts pulsate, their mutual attraction and connection to love magic ignites. Mortals experience it as new relationship energy that grows in connection and depth. Magics go through the same thing. Except we get a jolt that some of us are smart enough to recognize. Some don't." Donya held up her pad. She'd drawn a second set of intersecting hearts. One of the circles was dots and dashes. "This is when the spark fails to ignite or isn't the right connection."

"Is this what happened to Aprell and me when you tried to get us together?" Evan laid his hand on Aprell's.

Maxi tossed her pad on the table. "We tried matchmaking as we knew it. A few tarot card readings. Talking up how you two were close, knew each other, and share common experiences. A few love prayers happened, too."

"You bespelled us? Magiced us?" Evan asked.

Donya winced at Evan's tone. The accusatory part wasn't there a lot. The upset and hurt that had come through while he and Aprell were still finding themselves in high school and a short while after graduation.

"Evan," Tabby began, leaning forward. "No direct magic spells from us. Prayers and suggestions to Luna and the One, yes. Suggestions to you and Aprell, yes. Evan, Donya did her best to help you understand magic. So did Maxi and I. We learned from you, too."

"You did?" Evan took his hand off Aprell's.

"I learned from you, Evan." Aprell looped her arm around Evan's shoulders. "We learned about relating to mortals and them to us. You and I needed time to grow into ourselves and find us. Your mortal magic is medicine. I get what you're talking about cuz I work with mortal doctors and magic physicians. Without being around you, I'd not have the business I've got and the opportunity to expand here in Sylvan Valley. Thank you."

"You're welcome. I've got a question about something that happened while I was at Cauldron Falls." Evan tore a cinnamon roll in half. Took a bite and chewed. He wasn't sure he could explain what happened. He would try given what Abada had taught him about sleight of hand and what she said earlier about his great grandaunts' extrasensory perception. "I could sense what the magics needed for mortal healing. I almost could feel and read them before they spoke, if that makes sense."

"Partially makes sense. When your parents announced their decision to marry, the Witch Council wanted a genetics test." Donya didn't say more.

"Genetics test for what? Dad and Mom were both healthy up to the accident. Their injuries were severe and fatal. Not intimacy or having me." Evan started to stand, ready to pace again.

Aprell grabbed his arm and shook her head. "Hear Tia Donya out. My parents had to go through testing, too."

Evan slumped back against the couch. "Go on, Abada."

"Making sure that genes are compatible is important as you know. Fertility is part of reproduction. The Council felt then and still does that a couple should know their possibilities for having children." Donya sipped her coffee, wrapping her hands around the mug as she continued speaking. "Your parents passed with flying colors. The tests showed a latent trait that only a few magics possess. Extrasensory perception. The gene showed up in four out of the five tests the Council ran on your dad."

"This is what you mentioned last night about great grandaunts." Evan faced Abada more. "I got dominant human magic genes. Mom's intellectual genes and Dad's mortal dominant genes. What a mix, Abada!"

Donya smiled. "A mix that I'm proud to claim and call my grandson. You can find out more about the extrasensory magic trait in the Council's library. Mortal books have some inkling of understanding. The metaphysical parts of it are beyond my ability to describe them."

Evan hugged Abada and grinned. "What about Friday night? Are we planning something or leaving up to—" He leaned forward and whispered, "Mutual desire?"

Maxi burst out laughing. "Evan, I'm wondering who is chaperoning the chaperones after that remark."

Tabby stood. "Enough coffee. How about some lemon water and we eat a few of the cinnamon rolls instead of tearing them up?"

Aprell stood. "Gotta let out some of the coffee. I'm ready for a couple of cinnamon rolls when I get back."

Maxi rose. "Right behind you, Aprell. Be back in a moment."

Tabby put the coffee pot, mugs and spoons on the tray. "Donya, I could use your help, please."

Donya patted Evan's hand. "Think about what you could bring to a potluck dinner at Daniel Yost's place. We'll discuss this when we're all back."

Donya followed Tabby into the kitchen. "What help do you need? You opened the door and carried the tray in all by yourself."

Tabby emptied the coffee pot, put the mugs and spoons in the sink and laid the tray on the counter. She turned and faced Donya. "Have you thought about how Evans's going to take being on a group date with his grandmother and her boyfriend *plus* his extended family aunts and their boyfriends?"

Donya shrugged. "It's not like I don't look. I'm not encased in ice as a few on the Relief Society Council seem to think we elder magics are supposed to be."

"We're not. Maxi isn't either." Tabby filled a pitcher with ice, added lemon juice, and water. "How's Aprell going to handle that?"

Donya snorted. "How are Lucian, Mario and Daniel going to handle Evan and Aprell there? Or any of us? Did anyone figure this was going to be a one-couple-only date?"

"No, Aprell knows Daniel said he needed a head count on how many to cook for. She was here with me as we witnessed him and Maxi smooching." Tabby opened a cabinet door and reached for a glass.

"Tabby Nichols, you eavesdropped and spied on Maxi?" Donya clapped her hand over her mouth least she got louder.

Tabby glanced at her and nodded. "Yup, Aprell blushed and said good for Maxi. Now are you, Evan and Lucian on board? I talked with Mario, and he's fine. Said maybe the youngers could teach the oldsters a thing or two and vice versa. I got him to promise no strip poker, spin the bottle or other assorted naughties until any of us were home alone with them. Each in our own homes."

"Well, where does that leave Aprell and Evan?"

"At his place doing some of the same things probably."

Tabby clasped the glass she held with both hands. She lowered it to the counter and faced Donya. "*Misbehaving*?"

"No, wondering what is going on after all the niceties are dealt with." Donya took the glass off the counter. "We need four more glasses."

"So what are we going to do?" Tabby put four more glasses on the tray.

"That's what they're in there planning. Figuring out how each of us is going to break the ice and get to know each other better." Donya walked over to the kitchen door holding the pitcher of lemon water. "I'm thinking board games or a movie might work."

Tabby leaned closer as she got next to Donya. "Checkers and Chess?"

Donya snickered. "No, Building Bridges or maybe Who's Got the Broom or that who done it game. Movies might be a tougher decision."

"Abada," Evan began, taking the pitcher from her. "We've got a couple days before Friday night. How about introducing us to each of your dates over lunch or breakfast?"

Donya nudged Tabby. Tabby glanced at Maxi. Maxi shrugged.

"Evan, you got a good idea. Only issue is you are the odd person out. Tabby knows Mario. Mario knows Maxi and me." Donya filled a glass with lemon water and drank.

"Daniel's met Aprell and Tabby. He's been introduced to Donya and you briefly from my accident." Maxi took a cinnamon roll off the plate.

Aprell sat on the floor close to Evan, balancing her napkin with a cinnamon roll on it and holding her glass of lemon water. "Evan, how about a potluck dinner Friday night? We figure out some games we can play and a movie or two to choose from. A sorta family gathering."

Evan tossed the pad he held on the coffee table. "My list is short. It was introductions before Friday. Games and dinner or a movie. Twenty questions came to mind. Then I started thinking about what questions I don't want the answers to."

CHAPTER FOURTEEN

Thursday Morning

Evan rolled over, blinked and sat up, clutching the sheet tight to him. What was Aprell doing next to him? In his bed? In his apartment? How?

Aprell reached up and tugged at the sheet. "Do you mind laying back down or letting go? I don't like cold air. Thank you."

"Uhm," Evan lowered the sheet some. "Sorry about the cold air."

"Thanks." Aprell snuggled under the blanket and sheet. "What's got you shocked?"

"Shocked? Me?" Evan swallowed his next line. His brain babble wasn't going to cover his huh moment if he kept talking.

"Yeah, you," Aprell fluffed her pillow under her head and rolled toward him.

"Guess, I gotta ask, what you doing here?" Evan slumped down on his pillow.

Aprell chortled. "Not laughing at you. Laughing at the question. We came over here to discuss us and Friday night group date. It got late, and you were falling asleep. Instead of me going back, you offered a stayover. Now you remember?"

"Kinda. I got lots of questions popcorning. I musta been doing autopilot." Evan tucked the blanket sheet around him. Did he need to look under the covers to know if he was—oh, hell he mentally grabbed his conscience, told it to shut up and stop blathering.

Aprell patted his cheek. "Evan, you told your service you were taking the night off. You needed sleep. Recovering from the drive back and two twelve-hour shifts takes more than one night's sleep." Aprell slid her hand down his neck and rested it on his arm.

"Thanks. I remember talking with the on-call physician at the hospital before I hung up. My mind's starting to wake up." Evan rolled on his side.

"Glad I could clear that up." Aprell scooted closer to him. "Nothing happened except a couple of good night hugs and quick kisses."

Evan lifted the covers and looked down. He let go a long sigh. White and elastic greeted his gaze. His briefs covered him. He lowered the covers and raised his gaze. "Do I owe you an apology?"

Aprell sat up and shoved the covers down. Evan tried to look away. Flashes of neon purple and yellow mixed with oranges and greens assaulted his eyes and mind. Aprell was wearing his botched attempt at tie-dying t-shirt.

"If I stood up and turned around, you'd have no reason to blush. Though you are turning a nice shade of pink." Aprell pulled the covers back up and laid back. "You tossed me the first t-shirt you came to. Handed me a toothbrush and traveler's size tube of toothpaste and said I got first dibs on the bathroom."

"I hope I didn't give you an eye full as I got in bed." Evan glanced at Aprell.

Aprell smiled. "Showed me how you could shuck your clothes under the covers. You have a great escape artist trick going on with that."

She wasn't going to let on she'd seen him in his underwear as he came back from an early morning bathroom run. She'd probably flashed her dark pink bikini panties when she stood up and made her way to the bathroom. The soft glow of the night light reflected off the mirror over the sink and out into the bedroom.

"I'm glad we had time to ourselves. The last thing we sorta discussed was Tia Donya, Tia Tabby and Grandmother having boyfriends. We can handle them dating and companionship. When we got to more than that, we both shook our heads and almost said TMI at the same time." Aprell adjusted her pillow so she could see Evan better.

"TMI is the boulder in the room. Thank Luna and the One, as Abada would say, it ain't in the bed." Evan stretched and got more comfortable closer to her.

"Getting used to them doing things we did last night and might do this morning is going to take getting used to." Aprell moved her hand under the covers and laid her palm on Evan's chest. Warmth reached up, caressing her with each breath Evan took.

"Might do?" Evan lifted the covers and looked down.

"Are you saying you wanna?" Aprell stroked her hand up and down, stopping when she encountered the waistband of Evan's briefs.

"You changing topic?" Evan lowered the covers.

"Just taking notes." Aprell roved her hand partway back up close to Evan's navel.

"Note noted." Evan laid his hand on top of hers. "I don't think Abada, Tia Maxi or Tia Tabby would lie about doing this. I am not asking if they are. I'm going to say they are and let them have privacy like we're finally having."

Aprell nodded, pulling her hand out from under Evan's. She lopped her arm around Evan's shoulder as she moved tighter to him until she could feel his breath reach out and touch her face. "I want you. Been wanting you for quite some time. I gave up screwing a long time ago. I want a lover. I've longed for that lover to be you."

Evan stared at her. "You wanna be lovers?"

Aprell nodded. "Yes. Evan, you're part of me. Part of my heart and what I didn't understand was our connection."

"Heart magic is doing this?" Evan rested his hand between her breasts.

"Our hearts are doing this. Our connection has been and is strong. We get each other. We understand each other. It took us time to get to this point. We've wanted it for some time. Except. . ." Aprell paused, waiting for Evan's response. The next step was theirs to make together or not at all.

Evan rubbed his hand back and forth between Aprell's breasts. Warmth oozed through the material and onto his hand. Her heart beat steady and strong. Dr. Hauser had said during one of their lunchtime discussions that a strong heartbeat mattered. Knowing a person you cared about was healthy alleviated concerns. That was why teens waited to go on their first wild hunt and transmorph combined. Health mattered. Concern and caring mattered. From the moment he and Aprell reunited, there was a connection reigniting. A confidence in each of them knowing who they were, what they were capable of and sure of their place in their world.

"Aprell, I admit you been on my mind from the moment I took Tia Maxi to the emergency room. And it wasn't all about you as a caretaker." Evan cupped Aprell's breast. His thumb stroking close to her nipple on each upward swipe. "Ever since that bonfire disrobe, you been in a lot of my thoughts. Maybe a few fantasies, too."

Aprell's soft gasp warmed his face. Evan nodded, adding. "You're one of the loveliest nude women I've seen. I've seen quite a few."

Aprell tittered. "Evan, no doubt on seeing quite a few. I've seen my share of nude men since the bonfire disrobe. You continued to top my desirable list. Even most desirable since returning."

Evan cupped Aprell's cheek, rested his forehead on hers, and shook his head. "I believe desire happens. Chemistry happens. Heart magic seems to tap into both. The most desireable I'm skeptical on."

"Evan, are you telling me..."

Evan pressed his fingers against Aprell's lips. "Skeptical because I'm a hard science person. Need the facts and see things first hand. Not doubting what your heart—" He slid his hand between Aprell's breasts again and finished his thought. "What your heart tells you is right and true for you. I sense your desire and want from your pebbled nipples and the slightest female scent I am picking up each time I inhale."

Aprell shifted toward him. "We need to stop talking and start basking in the heart magic flames enveloping us."

Aprell pressed her lips to Evan's. She puckered and parted her lips a little. Evan's gaze met hers. He didn't pull away. His hand roved upward until he reached her shoulder. He slipped his fingers under the shirt collar. She inhaled sharply. Bright colors outlined her vision field. Evan parted his lips. The tip of his tongue tracing her pucker from side to side. His fingers tangled in her hair as he cradled her head with his free hand.

Sparks flashed. Bursts of firework-like colors. Roses, yellows and bits of mauve mixed with peach and reds. The colors she'd seen when two of her clients came for a reading. The colors had grown and brightened as one of the partners reached into his pocket and clasped his partner's hand. The proposal caught his partner and Aprell by surprise. The tears of joy, hugs and a loud resounding yes cut the session short. The couple embraced her and promised a testimonial plus an invitation to follow. She might not make it back for the wedding. Maybe Nancy could go in her place.

Evan pressed his lips firmer to Aprell's. The heat he felt as they kissed on the porch or hugged good night was a simmer compared to what sizzled inside him now. He didn't need to reach down to know he was erect. The tip of his cock rubbed against his briefs every time he or Aprell moved. Could she feel his wetness? Smell his pheromonal desire lacing the air. His senses heightened each time he touched Aprell. It was like he extended outward from himself, blending with Aprell's ethereal extension. Part of his subconscious reached outward, wanting to escape his corporal bounds. Evan drew back, breaking off the deepening kiss.

"Evan, is something wrong?" Aprell's words mixed with her scent and heat wafted over his face and downward onto his bare skin.

"Feeling like part of me is ghosty."

"Ghosty?" Aprell shot him a scowl and started to move away.

"Not the corporal body is done functioning ghosty." Evan rocked tighter to Aprell. It's like part of me is extending outward, reaching to mingle with you on all levels. Magical, ethereal and astrally. I don't know if I'm making sense."

Aprell kissed his cheek. "You do make sense. When crystal magic blends with heart magic. The ethereal parts mix with each other and take on a new phase of sensing. A new level of being. You're experiencing more of your psychic energy happening."

"It can slow down. My corporal parts want the physical enjoyment, too!"

Aprell pulled away, sat up and pulled Evan's shirt off. She rolled to the edge of the bed, stood and shucked her bikini panties. As she turned, she felt heat enveloping her. She faced Evan. He was giving her a few hot up-and-down gazes.

Aprell lifted the covers ready to get back under them. Evan tossed his share toward her. He arched his hips, shoved his briefs down and off his hips, past his knees and feet. He held them up, swung them in a circle and tossed them away from the bed. She tried to swallow. Her dry throat prevented her from saying anything. Her eyes lingered on the evidence Evan cupped. His erection.

"Touch me?" Evan asked, rolling toward Aprell. He kicked the covers away. There was no hiding. He craved her touch as much as his ego needed her gazes and verbal reassurances.

Aprell reached toward him. The bed dipped and bounced the two of them closer. One last move by both brought them not even a hair's width apart.

Aprell laid her hand on top of his. Her warm essence moved over him like a trickle of water making its first foray over its banks into new territory. He eased his hand out from under Aprell's.

"Evan, you're so soft and warm. Desire flowing through you, keeping you stiff and ready." Aprell squeezed her hand and stroked upward. Her hand stopped short of his glans. She leaned down, licking her lips.

Evan clutched what he could find, watched Aprell form an O with her lips and—"Oh, Blessed Luna!" Evan groaned.

Aprell flicked her tongue back and forth across Evan's glans savoring his salty taste. The unique mix reminded her of minimally salted potatoes. She took more of him in her mouth. Evan groaned again. His words unintelligible as his hips rocked toward her thrusting him in her mouth more. Lick, suck, and lick more. Up and down using her lips and hands to stroke and suckle all of Evan as much as she could.

Evan let go of the bottom sheet and mattress pad he clutched with one hand. He slid his hand along Aprell's hip toward the V where her legs met. Pubic hair, soft and thick, caressed his searching fingers. Further into the nest of softness, he probed seeking the physical evidence she was ready for his caresses and more exploration.

Wetness slicked part of his fingers. He found what he sought. Aprell was as excited as he was. Turned on as many of his medical school classmates referred to it. Wetness that increased as a result of a woman's arousal increasing. Evan stroked lower, seeking the pulsating part of Aprell's arousal. The external button that paired with caressing and rubbing as he suckled nipples could produce—His medical mind could shut off. Pleasure happened because both people were in tune with what was happening. One's energy and desire lit the other's desire fuse and kept the flame going both directions. Eureka, his medical mind crowed he'd discovered another aspect of heart magic.

Aprell applied more suction on her last upward suckle. Evan rocked his hips back onto the mattress and stretched his legs out. Much more and he'd orgasm. He wanted to do that inside Aprell. Mutual pleasure. Mutual orgasms, if possible. Part of him needed to taste his partner. Bring her small spurts of pleasure as he intensified the heart magic connection between them.

"I want to taste you. Smell your deliciousness close up. Lay back please." Evan pushed on Aprell's shoulders with both hands.

Aprell raised her head, still holding on to Evan. She carefully let go. He wanted to taste her? Oral sex had been a verboten topic between them in high school. Each had steered away from the pleasure topic many classmates discussed as their birth control choice. Back then, Evan and her weren't ready to admit sexual chemistry. They focused more on their friendship. Evan could taste her. Pleasure her orally. That still left birth control. He hadn't orgasmed yet. The thought of Evan jacking off left her feeling odd and empty. Birth control discussion, then tasting. They were heading to intercourse and a physical joining. Surprises nine months forward neither of them needed.

"Evan, before you taste me. We gotta discuss birth control. Who's responsible for it? What are we using? We know coitus interruptus is as reliable as the rhythm method." Aprell held her hands out in front of her.

Evan rolled over facing away from her. Had she killed the mood? Her heart beat harder protesting the break in the magic happening. Aprell leaned toward Evan, ready to touch him, when he rolled back holding up two items.

"Thanks for reminding me. I'm the one that reminds my patients about being responsible and protected in the heat of passion. Damn near broke my own rule." Evan scooted closer. "Condoms. Non expired. Before you ask or try to silently guess. Neither of us have been celibate. I had recent STD tests and checkups. Part of accepting the rotation at Cauldron Falls Hospital and keeping up with records at Sylvan Valley Hospital."

Aprell slid down, laying back against her pillows. She held her hand out, palm up. "I need to examine the condom packets. My piece of mind and knowing the info you have matches what I find. Sorry if I burst a bubble or two. I had a few clients come in with unplanned or unwanted pregnancies happening. Local health clinic class drummed into everyone, male and female, check condom packets, ask about what birth control meds, if any, are being used or implants."

Evan smiled. "Yeah, our medical brains demand info. Good for us."

CHAPTER FIFTEEN

Evan laid the condom packets in her hand. Aprell checked the expiration date on each. Good for three more months. She wasn't going to ask when he used the last one before now. Trust was hard-won at times. Evan's aura would show if he was lying. No black edges or areas that pulsed uneasiness through her. She handed the condoms back to Evan. "Keep them handy. I got a feeling we're going to need them soon."

Evan nodded and sat up. "In sight on my nightstand table." He clicked the lamp on showing the condoms lying in the glow of the lamp.

Aprell lay back, sliding lower in the bed. She spread her legs as she spoke. "Last medical checkup two months ago. No STDs. Been celibate for a while."

"Look forward to pleasuring you and sample tasting." Evan swung one leg over hers. Kept maneuvering until he lay on his stomach between her legs. His hands and fingers caressing her clitoris and labia as he spoke again. "Pleasure is my intent. If you're not feeling it, let me know. Your pleasure is my pleasure. We are both lovers feeding off each other's pleasure."

Evan slipped two fingers into Aprell, mimicking the movement he would be doing soon after tasting her. He slid his fingers out, held them to his nose and inhaled. Clean, aroused woman scents greeted him. He licked one finger then another as Aprell watched. "Just a teasing sample. Now for the appetizer."

He gently pulled her labia lips apart exposing her swollen clitoris. Evan lowered his head, lips open and puckered as he blew air over Aprell's clitoris. She rocked toward him. Her hands clasping his forearms. He slid lower on his stomach until he was close to one of Aprell's core pulse meters. He reached up, cupped her breasts, stroking his thumbs over and around her aroused nipples as he lowered his head and lapped. He copied his thumb movements with his tongue on Aprell's clitoris. Suckling her between his lips, he flicked his tongue faster. Aprell rocked tight to him.

"Evan! Ah sweet Luna! Yes!"

Salty sweetness flowed across his tongue and tastebuds. He continued lapping until Aprell loosened her grip on his forearms. Evan reached down, took part of the top sheet and wiped his face. Was Aprell ready to climax again?

He was ready to bring their physical intimacy into their mutual orgasm phase. Deep inside her, rocking both of them to one more orgasm.

Aprell opened her eyes, letting the room and Evan come back into focus. Evan lay between her legs, resting his head and hands on her thighs. He grinned, winked, and blew her a kiss. Part of her sat on the corner of the bed watching, waiting and smiling. Another piece of her astral projected over the bed, staring down, taking in the scene. Bits and pieces of her teen fantasies, homesick moments when she first arrived in Hawaii and found herself missing Evan, and the last two weeks knowing her heart had found the one she'd dreamt about, asked for and yes, even murmured prayers about.

"Wow, I think we hit the jackpot." Aprell reached up, rubbed her hand over Evan's cheek and sighed. "And that was just the start?"

"Uhm—yeah." Evan kissed her thigh as he rocked up on his hands. "I've got this to take care of." Evan cupped his balls with one hand while stroking his cock from the tip down to where his hands met. Aprell licked her lips. Seeing a man pleasuring himself and watching her enjoying it was intensely hot and sexy. Evan comfortable with her. Evan enjoying her watching him. Ready to take the chemistry and passion they'd ignited to an even hotter level. She fanned herself as Evan rose on his knees.

"Time for one of those mutual mind-blowing orgasms some people in our past swore we'd never experience." Evan balanced himself on his hands and knees as he made his way backward to the edge of the mattress. He carefully stood. His gaze still on Aprell. "You ready, sweetness?"

He paused not moving, intently watching and waiting. Waiting for the yes that said move forward. A signal that said time for a condom. Evan slowly exhaled, ready to say he was okay if Aprell wasn't.

"I'm going to confess something." Aprell propped herself up on her elbows. Evan flexed his fingers as Aprell announced her confession.

"We're ready." Aprell started moving down the mattress. "I know I'm ready. Are you ready?"

"The we says it all." Evan helped Aprell stand. He pulled her close to him, taking her hand and laying it on him. "I need inside you. Feeling you pulsating around me. Squeezing me as we reach that mutual orgasm. I know we can do it."

Aprell snuggled to him. All of her touched him in some way. His hands roved up and down, caressing her hips and buttocks. Her arms looped around his neck. Air barely slipped between them as they each took a breath. Sometimes almost in unison. Why was his blasted subconscious flashing him pics and text from all the sexual health manuals from his anatomy and physiology classes?

"There's a position that lets us," Aprell said, tracing the outer edge of his ear. "You game?"

Evan nodded, brushed his lips over Aprell's and stepped back. "Side by side?"

"Oh, that's one. But. . ." Aprell clasped him between her hands stroking up and down.

"Keep that up and we won't find out about either one." Evan clenched his hands, willing his thoughts to focus on Aprell and not the dang anatomy pics.

"Me on top is your best option." Aprell let go and walked around him. "Let's get you situated so I can mount you slowly. Slide you into me where the heat can envelop us more."

Evan swallowed twice. Watching Aprell walk away from him slammed him back to the bonfire night. Her hips swayed with their own naturalness. He reached out, patted each firm, lush cheek and scrambled onto the bed.

Aprell picked up the condom packet closest to her. She tore it open and faced the bed. Evan lay middle of the bed. His hands behind his head. Oh, how submissive he wasn't even though his position suggested otherwise.

"It's going to take both of us." Aprell tossed the condom on Evan's stomach. "If I fondle you much more, inside me isn't going to happen."

Evan worked the condom down and over him, pausing to check if she watched. Aprell nodded and knelt on the bed. "Good, you follow instructions well, slave."

"*Slave?*" Evan tried to raise up as she moved tight to him.

"Got your attention." Aprell put her hands, palms down, on either side of Evan. "I'm going to straddle you. Help me balance, please."

Aprell swung one leg over Evan's leg until she was partially astride him. Evan reached up, his hands on her hips. Aprell slowly rose on her knees, not quite straddling Evan. Rubbing her wetness on Evan as she did. Bestriding Evan was going to take teamwork. "I think I oopsed."

Evan slipped his hands up until he cupped her breasts, His thumbs tracing the underside of each as he spoke. "Wanna try on our sides?"

Aprell leisurely inhaled. She placed her hand on Evan's chest, over his heart. She could feel each beat and breath he took. Evan touched her in places she'd dreamt about, fantasized about, even uttered a prayer or two about, and today, admitted aloud where she wanted his touch. Going to the next level, actual intercourse—She exhaled and responded as her heart pulsed almost in time with Evan's. "Yes, on our sides as partners seeking our mutual pleasure."

Evan slid his hands back down until he reached Aprell's waist. He steadied her as she moved back over him. Massages relieved tension and soothed muscles. Aprell rubbing against him as she worked her way back to his side added new dimensions to pain and pleasure's closeness. He worried his bottom lip with his teeth hoping to distract his horny male id from pursuing a volcanic eruption a bit longer.

Aprell groaned, stretching out beside him. "Tantalizing as this may be, I need you inside me now. No more hesitations!"

Evan saluted Aprell, rolled on his side facing her and patted her leg. "Put it over me and guide me home. I ain't hesitating either."

Aprell rocked to him, placing her leg over his close to his hip. She clasped his condom covered hardness and rubbed up and down against him. Next rub downward, she rocked tight against him and. . .

Blues, reds, and yellows exploded around them. Aprell, her lips puckered, kissed him once. Twice and on her third rock toward him, she whispered, "Hold still. Let's soak. Savor the heat, heart magic and physical joining happening."

Evan nodded, unable to speak. He was inside Aprell as joined as two people could be without the astral aspect Abada talked about when she explained magics and supernatural mating. He could feel part of Aprell reaching out to him. His subconscious reared up, pulling the shade of his human eyes closed and opening his psychic third eye open. Evan remembered one thing Abada repeated about meditating. Slow breathing, focus on the moment and experience it mentally, physically and psychologically.

With each deep breath he took, his heart slowed its helter-skelter beating. His view behind his closed eyes cleared. Aprell and he lounging beside a wading pool came into focus as the vision expanded. Three toddlers played in the pool.

Evan couldn't tell if they were his and Aprell's children or a relative's. As the vision began to fade, a voice echoed through his psyche. "The future is built upon the now. Setting a firm foundation is essential to understanding do, grow and learn. Be optimistic and open to embracing the new you emerging."

Evan blinked as one shudder, then another rippled through him, thrusting him deeper into Aprell. He pulled back. Aprell rocked to him. Using a counter rhythm, they rocked back and forth as they found their sensitive spots they could reach. His fingers rubbing Aprell's clitoris. Her fingers tweaking and pulling his taut nipples.

"Oh, sweet Luna, I'm there now!" Evan called out. His balls tightened to him.

Aprell pressed tightly to him, groaning low in her throat. "I'm right there with you. Oh, Evan, don't stop now."

Except for the raspy breathing of two spent lovers trying to catch their breath and return to their bodies, no other noise filled the air. Evan firmly held on to the condom and himself as he eased out Aprell. He rolled onto his back and blinked until his vision cleared. He worked his way to the foot of the bed, stood and trotted to the bathroom. Checking the condom for leaks and a quick bathroom use were a priority.

Evan smiled as he checked the condom for tears or leaks. Nothing showed even as he filled the condom with water. No surprises nine months hence he hoped. Aprell entered the bathroom, cuddled to him, kissed his cheek and whispered the L word. He turned to ask what. Aprell put her finger on his lips, shook her head no and pushed him toward the bathroom door. Evan tossed the condom in the trash, rinsed and dried his hands. He paused at the bathroom door, holding out his hand as Aprell finished emptying her bladder. "I think we found that sleeping pill we were looking for."

Aprell's sleepy smile told him she agreed. As they pulled the blankets and sheets over their nude bodies and snuggled close, Evan wondered if part of his evolution was because he'd grown and opened up to new possibilities. Possibly, he'd stopped stifling his natural traits and opened a new door to accepting who he was, a bit magical, a bit psychic and very much a mortal, possibly in love with the person who knew him almost as well as he knew himself. She yawned in his ear, wished him good sleep and her soft breath warmed his neck as sleep claimed him.

Two Hours Later

Aprell blinked, opened one eye and squinted. Bright beams of yellow danced across the floor, up onto the bed and right across her pillow straight onto her face. Other times this happened, she'd had a dream vision. She blinked again, shifted slightly and smiled. Evan snored softly beside her. His t-shirt lay on her pillow where she'd tossed in her haste to undress. Evan's briefs lay on the floor illuminated by the sunbeam as it danced and shimmered as if the powers-that-be were attempting to tell her something.

Evan stirred, opened his eyes, nodded and flipped on his back. "Good morning I guess."

Aprell pulled the covers higher. "I can't see the clock. Whatever time it is, we need to get up and get on with the day."

"Why?" Evan kissed her shoulder. "A few moments more isn't going to hurt. I'm off. You're here. No urgent calls woke us."

"Here's why," Aprell rolled on her side, facing Evan. "How we going to explain being this late whatever time it is. We need to figure out what comes next."

Evan sighed. "Now you sound as bad as our grandmothers and Tia Tabby. Gotta plan and execute it. Does it all need to happen right now? How about we see where this Friday night group date, group gaggle or whatever it turns out to be go first?"

Aprell tossed off the covers, stood and stretched. "Probably a good idea. Come on, a shared shower ensures we don't run out of hot water."

Evan scrambled out from under the covers and hastily followed Aprell into the bathroom. Hot water, warm cuddles and kisses from the person his heart kept telling him as he slept was the one. His heart magic pair bond. His fated mate. Somehow those thoughts didn't unnerve or scare him like they once had.

CHAPTER SIXTEEN

Donya set six mugs on Maxi's kitchen table. Mario, Tabby, Maxi and Daniel were huddled around the fridge discussing what to fix for brunch.

"There's four eggs. Add some cream and cheese. Scrambled eggs." Mario reached for the egg carton. "Daniel, we could split the croissants you brought, put the scrambled eggs between them, and top them with a bacon and sausage mix."

"Ye got something, Mario." Daniel grinned taking the partial package of bacon from him and the three sausage patties he held out. "I can chop them like bits of salad mixings. Would ya add em to the eggs or top the chicken parts with the pork separately?"

"Eggs are eggs, okay?" Tabby placed utensils and napkins on the table along with the sugar bowl and carton of cream.

"Not to us sophisticated cooks." Mario pointed to him and Daniel.

"He be right." Daniel scooted closer to Tabby and whispered. "Think ye can handle the toaster hash browns without burning them?"

Donya pressed her lips together, looked at Lucian who shook his head and went back to prepping the coffee maker.

"Mario, I've never burnt a meal I've prepared for us." Tabby yanked the box of toaster hashbrowns out of Daniel's hand. "I can't help it if Maxi forgot to turn the setting down on the toaster oven at the community center. No one complained about the food."

"Aye, if any had Tabby dearest, would it have done any good?" Mario kissed her cheek. "The volunteers were the last ones to eat. A few said compliments to the chefs as they smirked and asked for more coffee."

"Okay, so I helped set the smoke detector off, and the fire chief grabbed the fire extinguisher. He didn't have to worry about traffic and coming across town. He was there eating and volunteering." Maxi shoved a frying pan and spatula at Mario. "Sooner you and Daniel get cooking, the sooner we eat."

"Lucian, there's more you gotta be able to help with than just cornering Donya by the coffee maker and turning it on," Tabby scolded as she walked past.

"I think change of subject is needed." Lucian set plates at each spot Donya placed a mug. "Aren't there a few people missing from this preparation meeting?"

"See Aprell, I told you our ears were ringing cuz they were gossiping." Evan pushed the kitchen door open wider allowing Aprell to enter past him.

"You'd think they'd have something better to discuss than us." Aprell hugged her grandmother, Tia Tabby and Tia Donya. "Good morning, Mr. Yost, Mr. Gomez and Mr. Chargena."

"Morning Ms. Aprell. Mr. Evan." Daniel pointed to the two chairs at the head of the table. "Your seats of honor await ye."

Evan glanced at his grandmother. "Abada, I hope you are behaving. Whatever form that is for the six of you."

"Well, Evan, are you sure you want to know?" Donya grinned and pointed at Aprell. "Seems your old tie-dye t-shirt does fit her well."

"Aprell, where's your shirt?" Maxi asked, moving closer to Evan and Aprell.

Evan shot both hands up, calling out. "Enough all of us. Aprell, I think you said something about putting your top to soak. I'll hold off the inquisition until you get back."

Laughter erupted as Aprell left the kitchen. Donya handed Evan a mug of coffee. "Sit down. Let the first half mug kick in before you try taking us six inquisitioners on."

Evan picked up the mug, sniffed and set the mug down. "That is strong. Who made it?"

"I did, young man." Lucian pushed the sugar bowl and cream carton across the table. "Maybe you need to punch it up a bit."

"No. Probably need water and an extra mug. This smells like espresso. I don't need a three-alarm caffeine buzz. Who are you?" Evan rose, made his way to the sink, and dumped part of the coffee out. He started filling the mug with water when his grandmother stepped between him and the gentleman staring at him.

"Evan, please take it down a notch." Donya glanced over her shoulder. "There's something I need to tell you. Could you step over here, please?" Donya pointed toward the stove.

Evan looked at Aprell. She shrugged and walked out of the kitchen carrying her top. Evan set his mug down and stepped away from the sink. "Abada, what's going on?"

"Gentleman you're quizzing is my beau."

"*Your what*?" Evan hissed.

"Evan, keep your voice down." Abada grabbed his arm, trying to tug him closer to her.

"Donya, mi amor, let me introduce myself." Lucian stepped around Evan, halting next to Donya. "You must be Evan. Donya's nieto. I am Lucian Chargena, your Abada's beau." Lucian held out his hand.

Evan turned around, walked back to the sink, picked up his mug and gulped part of the cooled potent brew. He set the mug on the counter and faced Lucian. "Glad to meet you, Lucian."

"Evan, why don't you see if Aprell needs help?" Maxi suggested, plugging the toaster oven in she placed on the counter next to Evan's mug.

"Tia Maxi, I think Aprell can take care of her top." Evan walked over to the stove and stood next to Mario. "I'll take egg cooking duty."

Mario grinned, handing Evan the skillet and spatula. "Basic survival cooking, right?"

Evan nodded. "I took over cooking my first year of med school because my roommates burnt more than what was edible. Local takeout place kept offering us leftovers."

Tabby sighed. "Let's get the rest of the introductions over with."

"Tabby, sweetness, not until Maxi's grandbaby is back. We don't need to repeat ourselves." Mario wrapped his arms around Tabby and hugged her to him. Tabby squirmed trying to break away. Mario kissed and nibbled Tabby's neck. "Stop acting like you don't like nibbles and kisses."

"Mario, cool ye down a bit." Daniel slipped his arm around Maxi's waist, snuggling to her. "We got cooking to do. Food cooking that be."

Evan set the skillet on the stove. He weaved a path between Mario, Tia Tabby, Daniel and Tia Maxi. He paused as he reached his grandmother. "At least you and Lucian have decorum."

"Oh Evan, decorum has many shapes, forms and degrees." Lucian sided up next to Donya. "Last night was a great testing and discovery one, wasn't it, mi amor?"

The kitchen door swung open, Aprell stopped halfway in. She glanced at the six older occupants. She let go of the door and made her way across the kitchen to Evan. "Good thing they didn't ask us about what we were doing."

Evan and Donya looked at each other. Their mouths moved. No words came out. Evan and Donya turned around taking in the group surrounding them.

"TMI! T—M—I!!" Two voices yelled. Silence dropped like a firecracker whistling through the air waiting to explode. Everyone quickly moved apart as laughter bounced off the silence setting off snickers, snorts and more titters. As each wiped their eyes and stopped hugging their sides, a lower degree of silence filled the kitchen.

Lucian moved to the center of the group. "Ice broken. Elephant balloon busted. Now, let's get brunch cooked. I'm famished."

Eggs topped with bits of bacon, sausage, and cheese a top two golden browned hashbrown patties accompanied by split toasted croissants slathered with butter and brown sugar sprinkles sat on each plate. Fresh coffee or tea filled each mug. Eight hungry adults gathered around the table. Hands joined as each offered their short blessing on those present and the food they were partaking. The clatter of utensils, yums and small talk enhanced the feeling as they ate and shared companionable questions and further introductions.

"Evan, Donya tells me you're a doctor." Lucian laid his fork and knife on his plate. "Specialty?'

"General Family Medicine." Evan leaned back in his chair. "You aren't looking for free medical advice, are you?"

Lucian laughed and saluted Evan with his mug. "No, wanting to know more about the most important person in Donya's life next to her."

Evan nodded. "I'm independent. Have a well run practice and am expanding my practice to include Cauldron Falls. What about your financial situation?"

"*Evan*," Donya exclaimed, setting her mug down on the table.

"Legitimate question given what I asked about." Lucian laid his hand on Donya's shoulder. "Evan, I own two bakeries in town. A third in Cauldron Falls and four more in Chicago with my partners, my brothers and sisters. Family of cooks and lots of family meals inspired each of us to open our own businesses. Baking is my forte."

Evan held out his hand. "Glad you're successful. I think we busted some of that leftover ice into mini chips."

"I agree." Lucian shook Evan's hand and sat in his chair next to Donya.

Daniel rapped on the table. "Miss Aprell, I got a large diner near the edge of town. Catering business and delivery, too. I no moocher. My house paid for, and I make salary."

Aprell leaned toward Daniel. "Mr. Yost, thank you for sharing. Grandmother is smart and checks people out before she lets them into her inner circle. You had to pass muster with her to get this far."

"Please, call me Daniel." Daniel smiled and shoved the plate holding the butter cookies Lucian brought toward Aprell.

" I will, Daniel." Aprell put her hand on the plate. "I'm full. Thanks for offering me a cookie."

Daniel pushed back from the table. He raised his mug. "Here's to the first familial eat. Maxi, love, thank ye for sharing your home with us."

"Daniel, you're welcome." Maxi started reaching for the empty plates near her.

"Grandmother, stop," Aprell said, standing. "Relax and let the rest of us clear the table. Family pitches in and takes care of each other. We can each put our plates and utensils in the sink."

Donya stacked hers, Lucian's and Evan's plates, putting their utensils on top of them. "Evan, would you put these in the sink, please? Lucian and I are going to get the pens and pads from the living room."

Evan took the stacked plates and utensils from her. He set them in the sink and turned back to the table. "Mario, Tia Tabby, Daniel and Tia Maxi, maybe you need to chaperone Abada and Lucian."

"Evan, who's going to chaperone us?" Aprell asked, rinsing the first plate and holding it out to Evan.

"Aprell, let's split the chaperoning. Ladies, we go get the pen and pads while the men folk do the cleanup." Tabby grinned and started toward the kitchen door.

"Dear ladies," Lucian began, slipping his arm around Donya's waist. "How about a fresh pot of Orange Marmalade herbal tea and some butter cookies?"

Evan grabbed the towel off the towel rack and spread it on the counter. "Gentlemen, dish duty is ours. I wash. Someone dries. Someone puts away while the others wipe down the stove, the table and sweep up the floor. Least we can do after Tia Maxi let us mess up, cook culinary scrumptious delights and offered her kitchen for our gathering."

Donya walked up to Evan, wrapped her arms around his waist and squeezed. "That's my grandson. I am super proud of you. Thank you!"

Evan leaned down, kissed the top of her head and looked back up. "Let's get the cleanup done. We got a Friday night potluck to plan."

Aprell kissed Evan's cheek. She whispered in his ear. "Don't keep the good secrets you can share them with me later."

Evan chortled. "I don't share what isn't mine to tell. Remember, doctors don't tell everything they hear."

"No fair." Aprell stepped back, adding, "I get it. Same with crystal healing practitioners."

Donya, Tabby and Aprell exited the kitchen. Maxi stood back, holding the kitchen door open. Daniel walked up to her. "Maxi love, ye need to trust us. We men can do this. No fights or problems. Go on now. Relax and get the conferencing area set up."

Daniel pushed her out of the kitchen.

"Do you think we should leave them alone in there?" Maxi asked, slowly backing away from the kitchen door.

"Maxi," Donya said, taking hold of her arm. "You've done your hostess work. We've played nice. Even began bonding in ways none of us expected."

"Yes, Grandmother," Aprell offered, patting the space on the couch next to her. "Let heart magic weave its spell among them. Let the camaraderie deepen and seek what level it can on its own. Male heart magic, as you've told me again and again, is its own blasted gender. Just like our female heart magic is sometimes overly feminine."

"All right. All right." Maxi dropped down on the couch. "I hope Evan doesn't get quizzed."

Aprell laughed. "Grandmother, I think descriptive details are not what any of them are interested in."

Evan filled the sink with dish detergent and water. He faced Lucian who stood nearby along with Daniel. Both held dish towels ready to dry the dishes he washed. "Lucian, how long have you and Abada been dating?"

Lucian smiled. "Off and on for a few years. Friends plus a bit more from time to time."

"I don't need all the more from time to time details. In this instance, Abada's privacy wins out over spilling all. I'm sure the more is well within adult perspective." Evan handed Lucian the first washed and rinsed dish.

Daniel moved around Lucian reaching for the next dish Evan washed and rinsed. "Evan, Maxi be worried about Aprell. She doesn't her hurt."

"Daniel, Aprell and I go way back. There's more than a casual fling happening. We're best friends in some ways. Pals in others. And family of choice for sure. Thanks for caring." Evan washed and rinsed several utensil pieces. He laid them on the towel on the drainboard.

Mario moved up behind him sweeping. "I think we all care about our lady loves. Tabby is getting used to me telling her I care. If I start to say the L word, she shuts me up."

Evan washed and rinsed the last plate and utensils. He laid them on the towel. He dried his hand on part of the towel and leaned back against the counter. "Mario, Daniel and Lucian, I hope you are okay with me using your first names."

The three nodded and paused what they were doing. Evan swiped his hands on his jeans and sat in a chair close to the table. "We're all here cuz we care. Aprell, Tia Maxi, Tia Tabby and Abada care as well. It's where we go from here individually that matters plus as a group." Evan held up his hand. "Are we in this together?"

Daniel high-fived him first. He stacked the dried dishes on the table. "Dinner Friday night at my place. Got a big eat-in kitchen and beef stew basics."

Mario high-fived Evan next after drying the utensils and placing them next to the plates. "I'll make a rum layer cake and bring my ice cream churn. Homemade ice cream is great with the cake."

Lucian hung up the dish towels, held the dustpan for Mario, and dumped the dustpan in the trashcan near the back door. He handed the dustpan to Mario. Lucian held up both hands. "Double high five happening, Evan. One for your spearheading our first joint work detail. Second, for you accepting Donya and I are a couple."

Evan double high-fived Lucian. "Okay, I'll bring the ice cream makings, Daniel. Mario, you bring the toppings, please. And Daniel, what can Lucian kick in?"

"Some of his homemade biscuits or yeast rolls and cinnamon butter." Daniel grinned and pointed to Lucian. " Ye be okay with that, Lucian?"

"Yes, and a couple bottles of wine from my eldest sister's vineyard. Zinfedal goes well with any meal. Homecooked enhances the flavor." Lucian pulled out his cell phone. "Let me add these to my Friday date night reminder."

"Sounds like we got the basics covered. We'll let the *women* decide the rest." Evan chuckled knowing Abada and the rest would chastise him for describing them as women rather than using their names.

CHAPTER SEVENTEEN

Daniel swung the kitchen door open. Lucian exited first. Mario followed next. Evan stopped closer to Daniel. "Go on. I'll hold this."

Daniel nodded and exited the kitchen. Evan waited until his grandmother, Aprell, Tia Tabby and Tia Maxi looked up. "Women—er—I mean ladies. We're back. How much have you decided on Friday night?"

Aprell crossed the room, stopping when she was toe to toe with him. "We've decided strip poker might be a good idea for Friday after dinner game time."

"I think we'd do better taking all the spare board game parts we found clearing out the donation bin at the thrift store. Make up our own game. And the questions you have to truthfully answer to move around the board." Mario grinned and nudged Tabby.

"Are you saying we lie?" Tabby folded her arms across her chest. "Mario Gomez, what have you lied to me about?"

Donya shook her head and knocked on the end table next to the couch. "Enough sarcasm."

Maxi held up her pad, turning it so everyone could see it. "Our list goes like this. Gather at Daniel's at seven. Cook dinner from seven-thirty to eight. Eight to nineish eat dinner. Clean up and everyone chaperones themselves home."

Daniel sat on the arm of the chair Maxi sat in. "Problem is we figured out what each of us is bringing. Beef stew is easy makings. I'm covering that."

Lucian sat next to Donya. "I'm bringing two bottles of Estella's Zinfedal circa 2021. Fresh made cinnamon butter and two dozen of my yeast biscuits."

"I've got the ice cream makings to accompany Mario's Rum Sponge Cake." Evan crouched near the chair Aprell sat in. "We figured you ladies could handle the appetizers, sides like a salad or two. You know nothing too hard. Besides looking pretty and heading up the games after dinner."

Three pads flew in Evan's direction. Two landed close to his feet. The third bounced off his shoulder and fell next to the others.

Evan gulped. He glanced at each of his male counterparts. They shrugged. Aprell picked up her pad and marched across the room, shaking it until she was toe to toe with him. "We heard the *women* remark loud and clear."

"Eavesdropping at the door?" Lucian asked, facing Donya. "Mi amor, you don't trust us?"

Donya poked Lucian as she spoke. "*Trust* has nothing to do with pejorative words like *women* and *ladies* when you say them empathically. How does you *men* or *dudes* sound?"

Lucian stood, pulled the waistband of his jeans forward and glanced downward. "From what I can see, dude and men is what I am. How about you Evan? Daniel? Mario?"

Evan grabbed Aprell's arm, tugged her to him and called out, "I love your teasing and kidding. I also love you, Aprell Stallings."

"Evan, don't kid me like that." Aprell pushed against Evan. She leaned closer, whispering, "This prank didn't work in high school. It isn't going to work now."

"Aprell, what makes you think I'm pranking you?" Evan brushed his lips over Aprell's and stepped back. "I'm not pranking you. I declared I love you."

"Hey Evan," Mario said, stepping around him and Aprell. "Perhaps if the rest of us men folk declare our feelings, our ladies will know we're telling the truth."

"Mario Gomez, I am not your *lady*!" Tabby stood up.

"What are you then?" Mario asked making his way to where Tabby stood. "Girlfriend isn't adult enough. Or age appropriate."

"Are you calling me old?" Tabby put her hands on her hips.

Mario looped his arm around one of Tabby's. "Tabby, you're my love. My partner. Care to spend the rest of our lives figuring out the details? The intimate ones we can negotiate later."

"Tia Tabby, I think Mario just proposed." Aprell moved away from Evan.

"I sure did." Mario kissed Tabby's cheek. "Who's going next? Daniel? Lucian?"

"I am," Donya declared as she patted the space on the couch next to her. "Lucian, get yourself over here, please."

Lucian glanced at Evan, Mario and Daniel. He shrugged and made his way to the couch. "Donya, mi amor, you aren't the dominant in this relationship."

"Lucian Chargena, neither are you. One of us got to lead in this turn. And I'm doing the leading for our turn." Donya took hold of Lucian's hand. "We been dating off and on since Errol passed. You and he were best friends. You were like brothers. Errol visited me in my dreams recently. He said it was time you and I declared our feelings and set up housekeeping."

"Donya, are you asking me to move in with you?" Lucian tried to rise. Donya yanked Lucian's arm causing him to drop back onto the couch.

"Sure. Why not?" Donya pointed at Evan. "Evan, you got no say in this. It'll take getting used to."

"As long as I am not Gramps, I guess it'll work." Lucian grinned, raised Donya's hand and kissed the back of it.

Daniel perched on the arm of the chair Maxi sat in. He placed his hand on her cast. "Maxi, I'm part of the reason ye got this. Ye be part of the reason my grandson wears a helmet and teaches other kids skateboard safety. We been sparking and spooning as my great great grandma and grandda used to do."

Maxi ducked her head. "We done a few things more, Mario."

"Grandmother, TMI!" Aprell said in a loud voice. "Must you tell all in front of everyone?"

"What am I telling?" Maxi scooted to the edge of her chair. "Aprell, Daniel and I been talking and sorta dating for a few months. It's time I share with you, Donya, Tabby, Evan and the rest, especially Daniel, how I feel."

Aprell slumped in her chair. She glanced at Evan who stood next to her.

"Aprell, it's okay. Tia Maxi's got all of us. You don't need to worry when you go back to Hawaii." Evan clasped Aprell's hand.

"Evan, there's something I need to tell you." Aprell tried to pull her hand away.

"Aprell, let me go first, please." Maxi picked up the folder off the end table next to her chair. "Daniel asked me to move in with him several months ago. I wasn't ready to let go of the house. I wanted it here for if you came home. Now you are."

Maxi held out the folder to Aprell. "The house is yours even if you go back to Hawaii."

Aprell pushed off the chair and rose. She walked to the center of the group, close to the coffee table. She held up three fingers. "First, I'm happy for you Grandmother." Aprell lowered one finger.

"Second, Evan, I've probably loved you for a while. Just too scared to admit it." Aprell lowered another finger. "Third, I sold Nancy my share of Charms and Spells. I'm not going back to Hawaii."

Aprell lowered her third finger and held her hand out to Evan. He clasped it. She tugged him to her. "Heart magic is all around us. Heart magic multiplying as all of us are finding our heart's yearnings and longings. No other magic necessary."

EPILOGUE

The opening strains of a *Midnight Lover* by Shapeshifter Blues began as Maxi entered the circle of chairs middle of the Relief Society activity room wearing a pale yellow dress and carrying a yellow daisy bouquet. Donya and Tabby entered next wearing mauve and yellow floral print dresses. Their bouquets matched the tulip and iris flowers on their dresses. Aprell entered last wearing a deep red off-the-shoulder dress carrying a mixed bouquet of red roses.

Daniel entered from the opposite side. Lucian, Mario and Evan followed him. Each wore black pants and an off-white shirt with a red carnation boutonniere on the shirt's front pocket. Each of the men continued across the circle until they reached the center where Ralph O'Shay, Cauldron Falls and Sylvan Valley's Justice of the Peace, and his wife Tracey, Witches Relief Society High Coven Priestess, stood.

In the circle of chairs, three rounds deep, family and friends sat. Ready to witness four union blessings.

Ralph opened the binder he held and spoke. "Friends, family and loved ones, we're all special guests here. Special gatherings and union blessings are an integral part of Cauldron Falls and Sylvan Valley's traditions. These eight have come together to pledge a family oath and to pledge pair bonding oaths to each other. Let us begin."

Tracey faced Maxi, Donya and Tabby. "Do each of you give your witches oath to cherish, embrace and care for the men who are ready to bond with you?"

Each replied yes.

Tracey faced Daniel, Mario and Lucian. "Do each of you give you magical and/or supernatural oath to cherish, embrace and care for the women who are ready to bond with you?"

Each replied yes.

Ralph motioned Evan and Aprell forward. "Your vows are of a more traditional nature. Do you Evan, give your oath that you freely bond with Aprell to cherish, embrace and care for her?"

Evan took Aprell's hand as he replied. "Yes, I give my oath to cherish, embrace and care for you, Aprell. I also promise I will trust our heart magic now and going forward."

Ralph nodded and faced Aprell. "Do you Aprell give your oath that you freely bond with Evan, to cherish, embrace and care for him?"

Aprell laid her hand on Evan's. "I freely give my oath to cherish, embrace and care for you Evan. I also promise to trust our heart magic because no other magic is definitely necessary.

Ralph and Tracey joined hands and held their hands aloft.

"By the power of the state, the town of Sylvan Valley and the powers-that-be, you are mated, pair-bonded and legally wed. May Luna, the One and deities bless you now and always!"

Don't miss out!

Visit the website below and you can sign up to receive emails whenever Solara Gordon publishes a new book. There's no charge and no obligation.

https://books2read.com/r/B-A-RAUJ-SIHIG

BOOKS 2 READ

Connecting independent readers to independent writers.

Did you love *No Other Magic Necessary*? Then you should read *Blue Moon Valentine*[1] by Solara Gordon!

Returning home is never simple—especially when love, secrets, and unfinished business are involved.

Erick Cauldron thought he'd moved on, but Bianca Sylvan's unexpected appearance at a city planning meeting forces him to face his past. The budget issues are nothing compared to the emotional chaos they've stirred. Their complicated history is a powder keg primed and ready to explode.

Toss in Bianca's teenage twins, the mystery of their father, two matchmaking grandmothers, and an upcoming blue moon Valentine's Day—the chaos is more than just a budget problem—it's personal.

Can Erick and Bianca figure out where their individual missing puzzle pieces fit together, overcome their past and build a future together?

Read more at https://solaragordon.com/.

1. https://books2read.com/u/3GOnwn

2. https://books2read.com/u/3GOnwn

Also by Solara Gordon

Cascade Bay
Love Reborn
Reunited By Choice
Love's Triple Play
Three Hearts In Love
For the Love of Three

Cauldron Falls
Believe In Love
Home for the Holidays
Three Hearts Entwined
A Mate of Their Own
Moonlit Match
A Christmas Reunion

Cauldron Falls-Sylvan Valley Founding Families
Blue Moon Valentine

Peyton Corners
Falling for You
Caught by Love's Slow Burn

Sylvan Valley
No Other Magic Necessary

Standalone
A Heart's Desire
To Love You Again
To Love You Again

Watch for more at https://solaragordon.com/.

About the Author

Solara loves and lives with her partner of 21 years in the Metro DC area. What started out as a bi-coastal romance soon settled on one coast.

A vivid imagination keeps her busy creating her next fascinating romance. She enjoys creating unique characters and watching their journeys unfold. "Love freely given multiplies and will return endlessly" is a key aspect of her stories. Add in alternative lifestyles and her love for the paranormal, and the uncommon becomes the norm in many of her stories.

Her day job in the financial services industry pays the bills while she pens her erotic tales.

Read more at https://solaragordon.com/.

www.ingramcontent.com/pod-product-compliance
Lightning Source LLC
Chambersburg PA
CBHW030522260626
47157CB00005B/1849